Travellers in Time

Mysteries and Unbelievable Stories Throughout History

Maximilian Cross

DEDICATION

To all those dreamers who look to the past to understand the present and dare to imagine unsuspected futures. This journey is for those who believe that time holds more mysteries than we can comprehend.

Table of contents

Chapter 1: Introduction: The Fascinating World of Time Travel

Who hasn't dreamt of time travel? It is an almost universal fantasy. We have all, at one time or another, wished we could go back in time to correct a mistake or turn the clock forward to find out what the future holds. The idea of having control over time is something that strikes a deep chord in our humanity. But beyond personal desires, time travel is a concept that has captivated the human imagination for centuries. From ancient legends to the latest scientific theories, the possibility of breaking the barriers of time remains one of humanity's greatest mysteries and obsessions.

But what is behind this fascination? Throughout history, countless tales have been told about people who claim to have travelled through time. Some of these stories are so bizarre, so out of the ordinary, that it is difficult to dismiss them as mere tales. From mysterious disappearances to predictions of the future that seem to have come true, these stories force us to question: is time travel just a fantasy, or could there be more to it?

The truth is that the idea of moving through time, of altering what has already happened or jumping into what we don't yet know, represents something much deeper than a simple science fiction trick. It is linked to our most primal desires: redemption, curiosity, control. Time, as we know it, is relentless, and its constant advance cruelly reminds us that we are trapped in it. We can never go back. We can never get ahead of it. At least, not yet.

Time travel: between imagination and reality

Throughout history, stories about time travel have fluctuated between myth and speculation. Ancient cultures already flirted with the idea of beings who could move freely between the past and the future. In Hindu mythology, for example, there is the story of King Raivata Kakudmi, who travels to a heavenly realm and returns to Earth only to discover that many centuries have passed. It is a fascinating story because, in a way, it reflects that universal desire to transcend the limitations of time.

But of course, these are just myths, aren't they? The interesting thing is that, as science progressed, the concept of time travel began to take on a new dimension. With Albert Einstein's theory of relativity, we began to understand that time is not an immovable constant. Space and time are intertwined, and under the right conditions, time could, in theory, be malleable. This opened the door to new ways of thinking about what was previously just fantasy. But let's not get too far ahead of ourselves.

What do the stories tell us?

Perhaps the most intriguing thing about all this is that it's not just about science. There are accounts of people who claim to have travelled through time, and while many of these stories border on the unbelievable, some have left researchers scratching their heads. One man who mysteriously disappears after creating a device supposedly capable of manipulating time, another who predicts future events with astonishing accuracy, and then those who claim to have met their future versions.

The case of **John Titor**, an alleged time traveller who appeared on internet forums in the early 2000s, is one of the most famous examples. Titor claimed to be a soldier from the future, sent to our time to retrieve crucial technology for his time. While his predictions about the future have not entirely come true, some of the ideas he put forward have left many wondering if he really was a faker... or if he simply came from a different future than the one that awaits us.

On the other hand, the case of **Andrew Basiago**, who claims to have been part of a secret US government project called "Project Pegasus", raises another startling scenario. Basiago claims to have travelled into the past and into the future, even attending key historical events. Could this all be an elaborate fantasy or is there something more beneath the surface?

These stories, along with many others that we will explore throughout this book, have one thing in common: they challenge our understanding of reality. They make us wonder whether what we consider impossible might, in some corner of the universe, be possible.

Fantasy or reality?

The most fascinating thing about time travel is that it perfectly combines what we know with what we don't. As science advances, we discover more about the laws governing the universe, but we also realise how little we understand about time. Is it really immutable or, as modern physics suggests, might there be ways to "bend" it? And if so, are we any closer to discovering the secret of time travel?

For now, time travel remains a mystery, but one that offers endless possibilities. Not just for scientists trying to unlock its secrets, but for all those who dream of what it could be. We may never master it, or it may be closer than we think. Either way, the promise of moving through time, of seeing what we cannot see and changing what we cannot change, will continue to captivate our imaginations for generations to come.

1.1 Why are we so attracted to time travel?

Time travel has an undeniable magnetism. It appeals to us in an almost visceral way, and it's not just because it's a concept straight out of science fiction. It goes far beyond that. It is a profound reflection of our hopes, our fears and, above all, our innermost desires. At some point in our lives, we have all felt the frustration of the irreversible. Perhaps it was a decision that went wrong or a missed opportunity. From this arises the desire for a second chance, a way to go back and undo the mistakes, or even to go forward to avoid suffering.

But the attraction to time travel is not only a solution to our personal problems, but also a way to challenge the fundamental laws that seem to govern our existence. Time is a stream that never stops flowing. We are all caught in it, moving forward without being able to stop or turn back. We organise ourselves around time: we use clocks, calendars and routines to make sense of our lives. Yet it remains that uncontrollable element that governs our existence. No matter how hard we try to structure it, we cannot reverse or stop it. And that inability to control it is what makes it so intriguing. The possibility of breaking through that barrier and manipulating time is liberating. It offers us the promise of escaping the constraints of our own temporality.

A deep desire for control

One of the reasons why time travel is so appealing to us is our innate desire for control. We live in a world where so much seems out of our reach, and the idea of controlling something as powerful as time offers us a sense of almost limitless power. Imagine being able to go back to that pivotal moment when one decision changed everything. If you could make a different decision, how would your life change from there?

This power over the past and the potential to alter the future appeals to us because it allows us to imagine a world in which we could not only change our personal lives, but also history itself. However, behind this fantasy there is also a dark side. Having the ability to move through time not only opens up a world of possibilities, but also of fears: what if changing something in the past triggers unexpected consequences? This is where the famous **"grandfather paradox"** comes into play: if someone were to travel back in time and alter something as fundamental as the birth of one of their ancestors, how could that person exist in the first place? These questions feed our curiosity, but they also reveal the risks involved in the idea of altering time.

The irresistible curiosity about the future

It is not only the past that haunts us. The possibility of peering into the future is equally tempting. The future is an uncharted terrain, full of promise and possibility, but also fraught with uncertainty. We have all wanted, at one time or another, to look ahead and see what fate has in store for us. Knowing what the world will be like in ten, a hundred or even a thousand years is an idea that, on its own, arouses a mixture of hope and dread.

One of the reasons why travelling into the future appeals to us so much is because it might offer us a way to alleviate our greatest anxieties. If we could see how things will unfold, we could plan better, avoid mistakes, prevent disasters - or at least prepare for the inevitable. In a world where uncertainty about the future is a constant source of anxiety, the idea of "jumping" forward in time offers a magical solution to one of life's great mysteries: what happens next?

Time as a personal enigma

Time is not just a universal constant. On an individual level, each of us has a unique and personal relationship with time. It sets the rhythm of our lives: from birthdays to anniversaries, from future goals to hopes for what is to come. We measure everything within the structure of time. But, at the same time, time is something we feel but cannot control. We have all had the feeling that certain moments slip away too quickly, while others seem to drag on forever. This ambivalent relationship with time is what makes it such an irresistible enigma.

The desire to travel back in time does not only arise from the need to correct mistakes or to see into the future. It is deeply connected to our innate curiosity to better understand our existence. We want to know more about the past we did not witness and the future we will never live. In many ways, time travel is a metaphor for our desire to transcend the limitations of human life. It offers us the promise of seeing beyond our brief sojourn on this planet, of breaking through the barrier of the finite and the limited.

The moral implications of time

Altering time also raises moral questions. If you had the ability to go back and prevent a tragic event, would you do so? And if you did, what might the consequences be? Changing something in the past might prevent suffering, but it might also trigger unexpected effects that could be even more harmful. These are the questions that make time travel not only a fascinating concept, but also a morally complex subject.

On the other hand, there is also the question of whether we should really have access to the future. Knowing too much about what fate holds in store for us could cause us to lose the spontaneity and wonder of the unexpected. The idea that the future is already written is both intriguing and frightening. It raises questions about whether we really want to know what is to come, or whether it is better to live in uncertainty, in the hope that what awaits us will be better than we imagine.

This desire to control time, and the moral dilemmas it entails, is not new. Throughout history, various cultures have tried to find ways to understand or even master time.

A historical fascination

The concept of mastering time is not unique to modern science or science fiction. In ancient cultures, there were already legends of people who somehow transcended the boundaries of time. In Greek mythology, Cronus was the god of time, an imposing figure who represented the uncontrollable power of time over mortals. In Hindu mythology, stories are told of heroes who travelled to heavenly realms only to return to Earth to discover that centuries had passed. These narratives reflect our constant preoccupation with time, an issue that has been with humanity long before science began to speculate about the possibility of time travel.

1.2 From Fiction to Reality: Early Concepts of Time Travel

The concept of time travel, while it may seem like a modern idea driven by science fiction and theoretical physics, is actually much older than we imagine. While today we associate it with complex scientific theories and technological adventures, in ancient times there was already speculation about the possibility of altering or manipulating time. Mankind has always been obsessed with time, perhaps because it is one of the few things we cannot control.

Since the dawn of civilisation, human beings have conceived stories about gods, heroes or mythical figures who could move through time, either travelling into the past or moving forward into the future. In all cultures, from the Far East to Western legends, we find stories where time is not linear, but can be altered or experienced differently, creating a narrative in which the impossible suddenly seems possible.

Ancient time legends and mythologies

A prime example of this fascination with time is found in **Hindu mythology**, which is particularly rich in stories where time plays a central role. In the story of King **Raivata Kakudmi**, the monarch travels to a heavenly realm to consult Brahma, the creator god. What was a brief audience of a few minutes for the king, on earth was the equivalent of several hundred years. When he returns home, everything he knew is gone: his kingdom is forgotten and the people of his time have perished. This story raises the idea that time does not pass in the same way everywhere in the universe, a startling notion for antiquity and one that, centuries later, would inspire the theory of relativity.

In **Celtic mythology**, we also find tales of heroes who pass through mystical realms where time passes differently. Irish legends, for example, tell of warriors who visit **Tír na nÓg**, the 'land of eternal youth'. There, time seems to stand still; a warrior might spend what feels like a day in this place, but when he returns to the mortal world, he finds that decades have passed. These stories reflect a universal concern: the difference between human perception of time and the objective reality of its passage.

On the other hand, in the Far East, we find similar stories. In some ancient Chinese stories, immortals were able to live outside the normal flow of time. They would spend centuries in meditation or in a heavenly dimension, and when they returned to Earth, they would find that entire eras had passed. Legends such as these show that the idea that time is not fixed has been present in humanity since time immemorial.

A fascinating tale comes from Japanese mythology, with the story of **Urashima Tarō**. According to legend, Tarō was a fisherman who saved a turtle, which, in gratitude, took him to the Dragon King's underwater palace. There he spent only a few days enjoying the palace's hospitality, but when he decided to return to the surface, he discovered that more than 300 years had passed on Earth. Upon opening a box given to him as a gift by the princess of the palace, Urashima aged rapidly, as if time had caught up with him all at once. This myth raises a recurring idea in Eastern cultures: time can be experienced differently depending on where you are.

Similarly, in the Arab world, in the **"Arabian Nights"** collection of tales, we also find stories that play with the perception of time. In one of the stories, a man travels to a magical place where time seems to be suspended, and what was for him a brief lapse of time becomes years when he returns home. Although mostly fantastical tales, these stories reflect the human preoccupation with the mysteries of time and how it can be perceived or altered by forces beyond our comprehension.

Time as a philosophical concept in antiquity

The idea that time can be altered does not only appear in myths and legends. Ancient philosophers also reflected deeply on the concept of time and its nature. The Greeks, for example, divided time into two categories: **Chronos**, the chronological, measurable, linear time, and **Kairos**, the opportune time, that qualitative moment in which something decisive occurs, something that transcends simple chronology.

Plato speculated on the cyclical nature of time, suggesting that history was not a straight line, but could repeat itself in cycles. This philosophical thought influenced many later writers and thinkers, and even today, some scientific theories of time do not rule out the possibility that time has a cyclical rather than a linear character.

Moreover, in the Judeo-Christian tradition, the concept of time is linked to the very creation of the universe. According to the **Book of Genesis**, time began when God created the world, a radical concept for the time, when time was believed to be infinite and without beginning. This act of creation marked the beginning of time as we know it, but left open the question of whether it could be manipulated or altered by beings with sufficient power.

Mesoamerican cultures, such as the **Maya**, developed incredibly complex calendars, not only to measure the passage of time, but to try to predict the future. For the Maya, time was cyclical, with the belief that each 52-year cycle repeated itself in similar patterns, and this view of time as something that returns again and again has influenced the way we view historical cycles and the repetition of events.

The advent of modern science and the change of perspective

For centuries, these ideas about time were seen as philosophical speculations or mythological fantasies. It was not until the rise of the **Scientific Revolution** in the 17th century that time began to be studied from a scientific point of view. **Isaac Newton**, one of the fathers of modern physics, was the first to propose that time was absolute and linear, a universal constant that moved uniformly, regardless of what was happening in the universe. In his view, time flowed like a river, unstoppable and always in the same direction.

This idea of Newton's prevailed for centuries, shaping our understanding of time in all areas of knowledge. However, in the 20th century, **Albert Einstein** turned this view upside down with his **theory of relativity**. Einstein showed that time is not an immutable constant, but can expand or contract depending on the speed at which an object is moving or the influence of gravity.

Time dilation: the science that proves the theory

Although time dilation may seem an abstract concept, modern science has proven its existence in several experiments. One of the best known is the experiment with atomic clocks on board aeroplanes. In 1971, the **Hafele and Keating** experiment was conducted, where atomic clocks were sent on commercial aircraft flying in opposite directions around the Earth. The results showed a small but detectable difference in elapsed time compared to identical clocks on the Earth's surface. Such experiments show that time is not a fixed constant; it can slow down when objects move at high speeds, as predicted by the theory of relativity.

Time dilation is even more visible in space. Probes and satellites orbiting the Earth at high speed also experience this difference in time perception. In fact, GPS satellites, which rely on extremely accurate clocks, must correct for these time differences to provide an accurate location.

Without these corrections, location error would quickly accumulate, causing large deviations.

Wormholes and the possibility of time travel

Einstein not only altered our perception of time, but also laid the groundwork for another intriguing idea: **wormholes**. These hypothetical shortcuts through space-time, predicted by general relativity, could allow someone to travel not only great distances in space, but also in time. Although no empirical evidence for the existence of such tunnels has yet been found, the possibility has intrigued scientists and science fiction writers alike.

For a wormhole to function as a time portal, many physicists believe we would need something called **exotic matter**, a type of matter that could generate negative energy and allow the wormhole to stay open. Exotic matter remains a mystery, but its mere possibility opens up a host of questions about the structure of time and space. Although we have not yet found this matter, in theory, it could provide the key to making time travel a reality.

Moreover, even if we were to find this matter, there is a risk that wormholes are unstable. They could collapse before anyone could travel through them, destroying everything inside. Still, the idea remains a subject of fascination for scientists and science fiction writers alike.

The legacy of science fiction in the concept of time travel

While science has given us a more solid basis for thinking about the possibility of time travel, science fiction has been the real spark that has kept the idea alive in the collective imagination. Time travel has allowed writers and filmmakers to explore themes of morality, destiny and the impact of our actions, questioning what would happen if we had the power to alter time.

Closing

With the evidence of time dilation and wormhole theories, time travel seems to be closer to the realm of possibility. But do we really want to open that door, are we prepared for the consequences that time manipulation might bring, or are some things better left undiscovered?

1.3 Time travel in science fiction: H.G. Wells and beyond

It is impossible to talk about time travel without mentioning H.G. Wells. His novel THE TIME MACHINE (1895) not only pioneered the genre, but also ignited a spark that would light up the imagination of entire generations. Before Wells, the idea of time travel was little more than a vague dream, a fantasy in ancient legends and mythologies. But Wells not only gave us a machine to navigate the ages, he also posed unsettling questions that, more than a century later, we are still trying to answer.

H.G. Wells: A pioneer ahead of his time

When THE TIME MACHINE was published, the world was still digesting the Industrial Revolution, and concepts such as time travel seemed much more fantasy than science. Yet Wells had a visionary ability that allowed him to blend science and speculation in a way that was surprisingly compelling for his time. It is no coincidence that he is often considered one of the founding fathers of modern science fiction.

What is fascinating about Wells is how he uses a simple invention - a time machine - as a vehicle to explore much deeper themes. Rather than just telling a story about adventures in the past or the future, he makes us question the very nature of time and the fate of humanity. The journey taken by its protagonist is not simply a journey through the ages of history, but a journey into the very heart of humanity's evolution and decay.

The social and philosophical context of The Time Machine

It is important to remember the context in which H.G. Wells wrote THE TIME MACHINE. In the late 19th century, society was deeply influenced by Darwin's evolutionary theories, and this is reflected in the bleak future that Wells imagines. In his novel, Wells does not present a bright, technological future, but one in which humanity has degenerated into two species: the Eloi and the Morlocks. The Eloi, a weak and passive race, are the result of a future where humanity has lost its ingenuity and determination, while the Morlocks represent a working class that has been driven underground, adapting to the darkness and becoming a primitive and brutal force.

This bleak vision of the future is not only a commentary on the fate of humanity, but also a reflection on the deep social divisions of Wells' time.

At a time of great social inequalities, THE TIME MACHINE is both a warning and a critique of the extremes of industrialisation and capitalism. Wells suggests that, without a change in the power structure, humanity is destined for eventual decline.

But where does this critical view come from? **The life of H.G. Wells** may provide some clues. Born into a working-class family, Wells experienced at first hand the social differences of Victorian England. After several attempts to improve his situation, Wells immersed himself in writing, where he found a means of channelling his observations about society and his concerns about the future. His scientific education, which included studies in biology under the tutelage of Thomas Huxley (an advocate of Darwin's theories), also had a profound influence on his work. It is not difficult to see how these influences led Wells to imagine a future where class tensions and biological evolution converge in a disturbing picture of the fate of humanity.

Wells versus other contemporary authors

H.G. Wells was not the only writer of his time to dream of the future, but he was certainly one of the most daring in his approach to time. Authors such as **Jules Verne** and **Edward Bellamy** also explored the future in their works. Verne, with his more optimistic style, imagined technological adventures that challenged the limits of the present in works such as FROM THE EARTH TO THE MOON and TWENTY THOUSAND LEAGUES UNDER THE SEA. On the other hand, Bellamy, in LOOKING BACKWARDS, presented a more utopian vision of the future, where social inequalities had been eliminated.

What distinguishes Wells from these authors, however, is his willingness to approach the future from a much more sombre and philosophical perspective. Whereas Verne and Bellamy focused on technological and social progress, Wells was more interested in exploring the consequences of that progress on humanity itself. For Wells, the future was not necessarily a place of hope, but a space of decay and conflict. While other contemporary authors saw human progress as the solution to the problems of the present, Wells suspected that these same advances could be the cause of future problems.

A Touch of Early Science: Time Before Einstein

Although today we associate time travel with complex scientific theories such as relativity, when Wells wrote THE TIME MACHINE, there was no scientific theory to support the possibility of time travel. However,

Wells was ahead of his time - in more ways than one - in sensing that time was not as rigid as it seemed.

In the novel, the protagonist describes time as the "fourth dimension", a concept that would later be popularised by Einstein's theory of relativity in 1905, almost ten years after the publication of THE TIME MACHINE. Although Wells had no knowledge of these scientific developments, his intuition was astonishingly accurate. Just as science fiction often anticipates scientific discoveries, Wells was speculating about a future that had not yet been proven by science.

In addition, Wells' interest in biology and evolution also allowed him to imagine humanity as an entity that continues to evolve and change, an idea that plays a key role in his vision of the future. Although time travel itself was a speculation, the future Wells described was firmly rooted in the concerns of the science and society of his time.

Far Future Intrigue: The Fate of the Eloi and the Morlocks

In THE TIME MACHINE, the vision of the future is not only a warning about society, but also a disturbing speculation about what can happen when humanity stops fighting for its survival. The Eloi, with their peaceful, carefree life, seem to have achieved a kind of paradise on Earth, but Wells soon reveals that this paradise comes at a price. The Morlocks, living underground, keep the Eloi like cattle, an image that disturbingly reflects the class dynamics of Wells' present, projected into the distant future.

This distant future is perhaps one of the most intriguing aspects of Wells' work, because it shows us a scenario where humanity is no longer the dominant species in the traditional sense. Instead of moving towards a utopia, humanity's future is one of fragmentation and regression. Wells forces us to ask: Is this the inevitable fate of humanity? Could evolution lead us to a future where the distinction between civilisation and barbarism crumbles?

Through the Eloi and the Morlocks, Wells poses a crucial question: **Are we destined for a future of decline, even if we achieve material progress?** This bleak vision not only challenges the optimistic ideas of his time, but also resonates with modern concerns about the impact of progress on humanity.

The Enduring Legacy of H.G. Wells

Today, the impact of H.G. Wells and his work is still palpable. His vision of a future where time is a path we can travel continues to inspire not only writers, but also scientists seeking to understand the secrets of space-time. Wells left a legacy that goes beyond fiction; he opened the door to a new way of thinking about time, not as an immutable constant, but as something that, in theory, can be manipulated. And while we haven't built an actual time machine - at least not yet - the exploration of this concept lives on in stories and scientific speculation today.

Time travel, as presented by Wells, remains one of the most captivating ideas in science fiction. It invites us to dream, to fear and, above all, to reflect on our relationship with time and the future. Wells, with his time machine, gave us much more than a story; he gave us a window into the unknown, and his influence continues to shape the course of science fiction more than a century later.

1.4 Time Travel in Film and Television: Entertainment and Speculative Science

Film and television have been largely responsible for bringing time travel from books to screens, making the idea accessible to millions of people around the world. In literature, time travel was more philosophical, even intimidating at times. But when the cameras were turned on, the concept exploded, filling our minds with thundering machines, dangerous paradoxes and completely insane futures. And who hasn't dreamed of jumping to another time at the click of a button?

"Back to the Future" and the golden age of time travel in cinema

One of the most iconic examples of this popularisation is, without a doubt, the BACK TO THE FUTURE saga. Marty McFly and his endearing DeLorean invited us to dream of the possibility of travelling through time as easily as we take a train. But BACK TO THE FUTURE also touched on deeper issues: What would happen if we changed something insignificant in the past? How would those small alterations affect our present or future? The film was not only fun, it also posed, albeit in a light-hearted way, one of the classic dilemmas of time travel: the BUTTERFLY EFFECT.

Robert Zemeckis and Bob Gale's script is full of thought-provoking moments: from the famous "sports almanac" to Marty's encounters with younger versions of his parents. It's a story that, while it takes liberties with the rules of time, never fails to remind us that the consequences of altering the past can be far more complicated than we imagine.

However, BACK TO THE FUTURE showed us an optimistic side to time travel. The consequences, though dramatic, could always be corrected, and Marty finally finds his place in a better future. Unlike other stories in the genre, this saga left us with the feeling that time could not only be travelled, but also controlled (provided you have a flux capacitor at hand, of course).

The Dark Side: Terminator and apocalyptic futures

But not all time travel stories are so optimistic. THE TERMINATOR is a great example of the opposite: the idea that even small changes in the past can trigger catastrophic futures. In James Cameron's saga, time travel becomes a tool of war: the machines send an assassin into the past to eliminate Sarah Connor, the mother of the leader of the human resistance. All this in order to ensure that the machines dominate the future.

TERMINATOR presents us with a more sinister vision of time travel. Here, time jumps are not to fix mistakes or avoid personal problems, but to ensure the survival of a race (in this case, the machines). Time is not a tool for entertainment, but a battlefield. What is most intriguing about this saga is how it posits the idea of a fixed future, a fate that seems inevitable: despite the characters' best efforts, doomsday always seems to be just around the corner.

In TERMINATOR 2: JUDGEMENT DAY, the question of whether the future is written or whether we can change it is introduced. "There is no destiny except the one we make", says Sarah Connor. But even with that message of hope, the film leaves us with the sense that time is relentless and that playing with it can have devastating consequences.

Beyond Hollywood: Dark and Time Cycles

Recently, the German series DARK has taken us even further into the concept of time travel, mixing the intrigue of time loops with a touch of speculative science and parallel universe theories. What begins as the disappearance of a child becomes a much more complex plot involving infinite time cycles and connections between generations that are destined to repeat themselves over and over again.

What's interesting about DARK is how it delves into temporal paradoxes without trying to simplify them. There is no "easy solution" here, no DeLorean that allows you to go back in time and fix things. DARK takes a more philosophical view of time, presenting it as an endless cycle in which, whatever we do, we always return to the same starting point. The characters are trapped in a labyrinth of decisions and consequences that lead them, again and again, to the same tragic fate.

DARK also dares to mix in elements of real science, such as wormholes, relativity theories, and multiple timelines. This kind of approach not only leaves us wondering about the fates of the characters, but also begs the question: What if all this wasn't just science fiction? What if there really were ways to move through time? DARK reminds us that, while the concept of time travel is speculative, science continues to explore these possibilities, and we are not that far away from turning fantasies into real theories.

More iconic examples of time travel in film and television

Film and television are full of fascinating examples of time travel. Some, such as Twelve Monkeys, explore the subject from a more psychological perspective. In this film directed by Terry Gilliam, time travel is mixed with psychology, and raises an intriguing question: Is time travel real or just a mental illusion? The protagonist, trapped in a time warp, struggles not only with the consequences of his travels, but also with his sanity, adding an extra layer of complexity to the story.

Another fascinating example is Christopher Nolan's INTERSTELLAR. Here, the director explores time dilation, a phenomenon based on Einstein's general relativity. In the film, the characters travel through space, but on different planets time passes at different rates. This adds a deep emotional charge to the plot, when the protagonist returns to Earth to discover that, while only a few years have passed for him, decades have passed for his daughter on Earth. It is a play that reminds us that time travel is not only a matter of science, but also of human emotions.

The film PRIMER is another interesting but much more complex example. This independent film, known for its convoluted plot, approaches time travel from a much more technical and almost scientific perspective. There are no flashy special effects here, but a thorough exploration of how small alterations in time can have huge repercussions. PRIMER focuses on the ethical and practical complications of being able to go back in time, presenting a temporal puzzle that leaves the viewer wondering if they really understood what they saw.

The psychological impact of time travel

Film and television not only explore the physical implications of time travel, but also its psychological impact. In DARK, we see how characters, trapped in endless time cycles, begin to lose a sense of their own identity and reality. The inability to escape fate and the knowledge that their actions may not change anything, causes them deep anguish and despair. Time travel, far from being a fun adventure, becomes a mental prison for them.

This theme is also explored in 12 MONKEYS, where the protagonist constantly struggles with temporal confusion and the loss of his identity. Time travel affects not only the outside world, but also the minds of those who experience it. In many cases, the characters face the existential anguish of being trapped in a spiral of unchangeable consequences.

The ethical dilemma of time travel

Another question that film and television have explored in depth is the ethical dilemma of time travel. If we had the ability to change the past, should we do so? Is it moral to alter history to avoid future suffering? In TERMINATOR, the characters must make difficult moral choices about who should live and die, knowing that any change in the past could unleash a series of devastating consequences.

Similarly, in INTERSTELLAR, decisions made on a distant planet have profound repercussions for those left behind on Earth. The characters must confront not only the laws of time, but also their own emotions, knowing that their decisions can change the fate of humanity.

Time Travel in Different Cultures: The Case of Japanese Anime

While Hollywood has largely dominated the time travel genre, other cultures have approached the subject in equally fascinating ways. In Japanese anime, for example, examples such as STEINS;GATE and ERASED explore time travel from a more emotional perspective. In STEINS;GATE, the characters discover that they can send text messages into the past, altering small details that end up having monumental consequences. The series, while entertaining, also deals with the idea of fate and the difficulty of changing it, as well as the fragility of reality itself.

In ERASED, a man discovers he can go back in time to his childhood, where he must solve a mystery to prevent a tragedy. In both cases, time travel is not just a narrative trick, but a tool to explore the emotional connection to the past and how mistakes can be corrected... or compounded.

More on culture shock: Paradoxes and effects that are part of our everyday language

Film and television have profoundly shaped our perception of time and how we interact with it. Concepts such as the GRANDFATHER PARADOX or the BUTTERFLY EFFECT have gone from being speculative scientific ideas to becoming part of everyday language, largely thanks to their popularisation in these audiovisual narratives.

The GRANDFATHER PARADOX is a dilemma we have already seen in films such as BACK TO THE FUTURE, where changing the past can create a paradox: if Marty accidentally interferes with his parents' meeting, how could he be born in the future? This idea, which might seem very abstract, has been brought to film and television so effectively that it is now a concept widely understood by popular culture.

Similarly, the BUTTERFLY EFFECT - the idea that a small change in the past can generate huge consequences in the future - has been widely exploited in films like THE BUTTERFLY EFFECT or series like DARK, and is now part of our vocabulary. We say that something has a "butterfly effect" when a small action has unexpectedly large repercussions, something that is no longer exclusive to science fiction films, but is deeply rooted in the way we talk about causality.

This kind of influence shows how science fiction, through film and television, has made us think about time in more complex and fascinating ways, incorporating these terms into our everyday language and, with them, the possibility that time is not as linear and predictable as we tend to think.

Time travel as a metaphor for modern fears

One of the most fascinating aspects of time travel is how these stories reflect the fears and anxieties of contemporary society. In films such as the TERMINATOR, time travel is used to avert an apocalyptic future dominated by machines. This dark future, to a large extent, reflects the fears of the Cold War and nuclear threat that prevailed in the 1980s, when the first film was released. Control over the future becomes a metaphor for the fear of total destruction, where small decisions in the past could seal the fate of all humanity.

Similarly, in DARK, the infinite time cycle in which the characters are trapped can be interpreted as a metaphor for the sense of inevitability we feel in the modern world. The sense of being trapped in repetitive cycles, where despite our best efforts we cannot change fate, resonates with the growing uncertainty about the future in an increasingly uncertain world, marked by global crises such as climate change, pandemics and social conflict. In DARK, the characters struggle against a fate that seems pre-written, reflecting modern anxieties about control (or lack of it) in our own lives.

This use of time travel as a tool to explore the fears of each era reminds us that science fiction is not only about imagining possible futures, but also about reflecting on present concerns. Thus, time travel becomes a metaphor for the human struggle to understand and, perhaps, control a future that often seems beyond our reach.

The Science Behind the Fiction: Wormholes and Quantum Entanglement

The most fascinating thing about time travel in film and television is how the stories have tried to integrate real scientific elements. Perhaps the best known are wormholes, which in Einstein's theory of general relativity could connect different points in space and time. These shortcuts, though not yet proven in reality, are a narrative tool that has allowed screenwriters and directors to imagine plausible ways of moving through time.

Quantum entanglement, a phenomenon in which two particles are connected regardless of the distance between them, has also inspired stories that explore the relationship between time and quantum physics. Although these concepts are difficult for even scientists to understand, in fiction they are used to add a touch of realism and mystery to stories, making us wonder whether science will ever really be able to explain time jumps.

Beyond fiction: Could time travel be real?

Film and television have turned time travel into a visual spectacle that fascinates and entertains us, but also leaves us with a question: what if it wasn't just fiction? Although we have not yet discovered how to manipulate time the way the characters in these stories do, science continues to investigate concepts such as wormholes and the theory of relativity.

We may not be able to travel in a DeLorean or stop doomsday like in TERMINATOR, but the possibility that time is more flexible than we think is still there, fuelling our imagination. And in the meantime, film and television will continue to show us possible futures, alternative pasts and the infinite consequences of playing with time.

Chapter 2: John Titor - The Future Traveller on the Internet Forums

At the dawn of the internet, when forums were the meeting places for the curious, conspiracy theorists and paranormal enthusiasts, a story emerged that continues to fascinate many to this day. We are talking about John Titor, a name you have probably heard of if you are interested in the mystery of time travel.

John Titor's story is one of the most intriguing in the digital culture of the early 2000s. A supposed traveller from the future who communicated on internet forums claiming to come from the year 2036. His mission, he claimed, was to save humanity from impending disaster. As time went on, his stories captured the attention of users around the world, giving rise to a series of debates, theories, and even a cult following.

But who was John Titor, what was it that he told that sparked such a spark in the online community at the time, was he a prankster, a marketing genius or, as he put it, a soldier on a temporary mission? The answers are unclear, but what is clear is that his story has left an indelible mark on internet forums and continues to be the subject of speculation more than 20 years later.

Below, we explore how it all began, what predictions he made, and the possible theories behind this enigmatic character. Get ready to delve into one of the internet's most iconic mysteries: John Titor.

The age of technological uncertainty

At the beginning of the new millennium, the world was at a technological crossroads. The turn of the 21st century had brought with it an unprecedented rise of the internet, and along with it, the birth of online communities exploring everything from trivial topics to theories that challenged reality as we knew it. This moment of global uncertainty, fuelled by fears of "Y2K" and rapid technological transformations, was the perfect ground for stories like John Titor's to emerge.

At that time, technology was beginning to become deeply intertwined with everyday life. The arrival of the internet in many homes forever changed the way information circulated, and with it, the way people discussed and questioned the future. This rise of connectivity, coupled with a cultural fascination with the uncertain future, was key to the popularity of a character like John Titor. After all, if technology seemed beyond our control, why not think that someone had already figured out how to manipulate time?

The myth of the traveller in popular culture

Before John Titor appeared on the forums, the idea of the time traveller had already been planted in the collective imagination by decades of literature, film and television. What distinguished Titor from other fictional characters, however, was the way he presented his tale: not as an epic adventure, but as a precise and cold military mission. This connected him more to the current fears of the time - militarism, government control, secrets hidden in technological projects - than to the fantasy time travel of the movies.

Moreover, the myth of the time traveller has always had a universal appeal. The idea of being able to move between epochs, whether to correct mistakes or simply to explore the past or the future, strikes a deep emotional chord. In this sense, John Titor was not just a technological curiosity, but a figure who embodied many of the human desires and fears about control over time and destiny.

The role of forums in the creation of modern legends

While legends and myths have existed for centuries, the internet enabled the creation of new kinds of myths on an unprecedented scale and speed. The forums of the time were very different from today's digital discussion spaces. Instead of fast and fleeting social networks, forums fostered deep and ongoing discussions, in which participants could interact for days, weeks or even months. These environments allowed stories like John Titor's to develop and evolve in real time, fuelled by collective enthusiasm and speculation.

John Titor was a kind of interactive narrator. Unlike fictional characters in books or films, Titor was "alive" in the forums, answering questions, giving additional details and adapting his story as users demanded more. This was instrumental in making his story not only capture the attention of internet users, but also in making it seem more credible. Just as old troubadours told their stories by adjusting to audience reactions, John Titor adjusted his story as forum users questioned him.

Forums as a space for belief

A fascinating aspect of Titor's story is how he illustrated the power of forums to generate shared beliefs. People didn't just come to the forums to read his posts; they interacted, debated, theorised and even researched collaboratively. Through these interactions, the online community helped shape John Titor's narrative, amplifying his claims and taking them beyond the confines of the original forum.

This leads us to reflect on how forums at the time served as incubators for new kinds of beliefs. Before the internet existed, rumours and conspiracy theories were transmitted more slowly, almost always limited by geographical boundaries or traditional media. With the advent of forums, these ideas could spread quickly and reach a much wider audience. This allowed John Titor's story to not only stay alive, but to grow in complexity and scope.

The rise of anonymity on the internet

Another crucial element that enabled John Titor's success was the anonymity offered by internet forums at the time. Unlike today's platforms, where users' identities are more exposed, in the early days of the internet most people used pseudonyms. This created a culture where stories like Titor's could gain popularity without the author's identity being questioned. This anonymity not only protected Titor, but also endowed him with an aura of mystery that only made his story more intriguing.

Moreover, the anonymity allowed users to become emotionally involved in the story without feeling pressure to reveal their real identity. This was instrumental in allowing many internet users to openly discuss theories and indulge in speculation, something that in a more "public" context might have been seen as ridiculous or fanciful.

Ambiguity as a key element of success

One of the reasons John Titor remains a talking point decades later is the carefully constructed ambiguity surrounding his story. Unlike other internet figures who claimed to know the secrets of the universe or to have had supernatural experiences, Titor offered a narrative that was full of technical details, but also strategic gaps. This seamless blend of information and mystery was crucial to sustaining interest over time.

For example, he never offered tangible proof of his time travel, but neither did he go overboard in promising the impossible. His explanations of the physics behind time travel, wormholes and gravitational singularities were not outlandish to the point of being immediately dismissed, but neither were they so detailed as to be easily disproved. Titor walked that fine line between the unbelievable and the plausible, allowing his story to endure precisely because it could not be completely disproved or confirmed.

The psychological appeal of the time traveller

Time travel is not just a technological or scientific fascination; it also has a deep psychological appeal. For many people, the idea of having control over time is extremely appealing, especially at a time when global uncertainty was at its height. Being able to go back and correct mistakes, or to go forward to see what the future holds, represents a way of escaping human limitations. The time traveller embodies this universal yearning: to break free from the constraints of the present and rewrite destiny.

John Titor, with his mission from the future, embodied this desire for control over time. He was not just any traveller; he was someone who had a specific purpose, a mission that, in his telling, could alter the future of all humanity. By linking his narrative to political, technological and war events, he offered a version of the future that resonated deeply with the fears and concerns of his audience. But interestingly, he never tried to sell the idea of a utopian future. His narrative was bleak, which made it all the more intriguing and believable for an audience that was already prepared to believe in dystopian scenarios.

The figure of the soldier-traveller in contemporary culture

It is curious that John Titor did not present himself as a scientist or a solitary genius, but as a soldier. In the collective imagination, the figure of the soldier has been associated with obedience, discipline and sacrifice. This choice of identity was not accidental: by presenting himself as part of a secret military operation, Titor was appealing to one of the oldest and most persistent conspiracy theories in modern history, that of the government withholding information about advanced technologies and clandestine experiments.

In this sense, Titor was not just a time traveller, but a cog in the wheel of a futuristic military machine operating in secret. This gave his story an additional level of credibility for those already predisposed to believe in the existence of top-secret military programmes. Theories about Area 51, the HAARP project and CIA covert operations were already part of the popular imagination in the 2000s, and Titor was able to exploit this context to make his story more plausible.

Emotional connection with the audience

Beyond the technical details and the coherence of his story, John Titor's success was largely due to the emotional connection he made with his audience. Forum users saw Titor not just as a teller of an intriguing story, but as someone who was sharing vital information about the future of humanity. This made Titor more than just a fictional character: he became a kind of digital prophet, someone who warned of dangers lurking on the horizon.

Many users interacted with Titor not only to question his story, but also to seek answers about their own future. Titor's talk of war, technological catastrophe and a dystopian future resonated with a generation that grew up in the midst of the Cold War, the fear of nuclear weaponry and the uncertainties of the digital age. Titor's answers, though sometimes vague, gave the sense that there was a plan in place, a way to deal with this uncertain future.

The endurance of the Titor myth

It is curious to think that, more than 20 years after its appearance, John Titor's story continues to generate interest. This is not only a testament not only to the story itself, but to the power of internet narratives to transcend time. Despite the fact that many of his predictions did not come true (as will be explored below), the figure of Titor has managed to remain relevant. This is partly because his story is not just about future events or failed predictions, but about something deeper: the human desire to understand time, to control destiny and to imagine possible futures.

Technological uncertainty as a trigger for speculation

The beginning of the 21st century brought with it a fascination with technological possibilities and at the same time a growing concern about their consequences. By the end of the 1990s, panic over the dreaded "Y2K" computer failure had caused people to begin to look with suspicion at advances that had once been celebrated. The turn of the millennium was marked by duality: hope and fear. This atmosphere of uncertainty was crucial to the emergence of modern legends such as John Titor.

Conversations about time travel, until then mainly the domain of science fiction, began to become part of more serious discussions on internet forums where people allowed themselves to imagine, but also to question, whether we were really close to discovering the keys to manipulating time. Titor appeared at a time when humanity was beginning to confront the limits of its control over new technologies, and his account provided a new angle to that discussion: the idea that the technology of the future could not only fail, but have catastrophic consequences.

The state of science and the physics of time

While time travel was still in the realm of the hypothetical in modern science, by the late 1990s and early 2000s, there was already a growing interest in physical theories that suggested that time was not as immutable as previously thought. Concepts such as Einstein's theory of relativity and wormholes offered a theoretical basis for the possibility of travelling through time, putting a new spin on popular conversations.

To an audience that was beginning to be more exposed to these ideas through science documentaries, popular science programmes and, of course, the popularisation of science fiction in film, Titor's ideas about the possibility of travelling between timelines no longer sounded so far-fetched. In fact, his ability to articulate these ideas with a clarity that seemed scientific was one of the key factors that made his account stand out from the many other stories circulating on the internet at the time. Titor's explanations seemed to be well aligned with the most advanced theoretical developments on the nature of time and space.

The role of the internet as a channel for stories and mysteries

The internet, in its early years, was a less regulated and far more mysterious space than it is today. The early forums and chat rooms, where John Titor's story took shape, were places where speculation and conspiracy theories could flourish without the constraints imposed by traditional institutions of knowledge or scientific authorities. Users of these online spaces were open to radical theories and to exploring ideas that, in other settings, would be quickly rejected.

It was this that allowed stories like John Titor's to not only survive, but to be fuelled by the enthusiasm and doubts of the online community. People who interacted with Titor, as well as those who simply followed the conversation from the outside, saw these forums as spaces of freedom where the impossible could be debated without the constraints of the real world.

Moreover, Titor's narrative was not limited to a simple story, but unfolded in real time, allowing users to feel that they were part of a kind of collective social experiment. This constant interaction between the supposed time traveller and the users was crucial for the story to maintain its relevance. In many ways, the internet became the fertile ground where a new form of contemporary mythology began to germinate.

The phenomenon of the digital prophet

John Titor, beyond being an interactive storyteller, was seen by some as a kind of "digital prophet". Rather than sharing his knowledge from a place of authority or power, he did so from a pseudonym in a forum, a place where anyone could participate and have their say. However, the warnings he offered about the future had an almost messianic resonance. He warned of impending catastrophes, both political and technological, and described a dystopian future that reflected many of the fears of the time.

This role of "digital prophet" was amplified because, unlike other public figures or theorists talking about the future, Titor interacted directly with his audience. He could answer questions, adjust details of his story and offer new pieces of information in real time, which reinforced the sense of authenticity. He wasn't just someone who would throw out a prediction and disappear; he was available to those who wanted to know more or challenge his claims. And this direct connection with the audience made his story even more compelling.

The appeal of the dystopian future at the turn of the millennium

Another important reason why John Titor's story resonated so strongly was the cultural fascination with dystopian futures at the time. Films such as **"The Matrix"** and **"Terminator"** had already familiarised audiences with the idea of a bleak future, where technological advances did not necessarily bring progress, but chaos and destruction. Titor tapped into this cultural climate by depicting a future where the United States had been torn apart by civil war and the world was on the brink of collapse after a nuclear conflict.

This apocalyptic vision not only aroused fear, but also a kind of attraction to the inevitable. In the mindset of the time, with the 9/11 attacks and the War on Terror just around the corner, many people felt that the dystopian future Titor described was, in a sense, plausible. This led them to wonder whether his warnings might be a real vision of what was to come after all.

The resonance of technological warnings

In his account, John Titor spoke of a mission that involved retrieving an IBM 5100 computer to avert a technological disaster in his timeline. What was interesting about this statement was not only the specificity of the device, but what it implied: that the technological problems of the future would not be caused by a lack of progress, but by the obsolescence of certain critical tools of the past. This concept resonated with those who were already familiar with the Y2K problem, where a glitch in computer code could have caused global chaos.

Moreover, the idea that a seemingly antiquated piece of technology could be vital to the future added a layer of credibility to Titor's story. Rather than relying on implausible futuristic technologies, Titor was describing a scenario in which technological solutions were deeply connected to the past, giving his account an unexpected sense of realism.

2.1 The story that began in the forums

Imagine it is the year 2000. The Internet is starting to become part of everyday life, but it is still a wild space where information runs unchecked, where rumours and extraordinary stories can grow without anyone interrupting them too quickly. There are no social media giants as we know them today; there is no algorithm controlling what you see. In those days, forums are the digital corners where curious minds and seekers of the unknown gather to exchange ideas, theories, and even their fears.

Forums at the turn of the millennium were, in many ways, spaces of creative freedom and, at the same time, of informational chaos. There was no rigorous control of content and any user could post pretty much whatever they wanted. It was the perfect breeding ground for conspiracy theories, paranormal phenomena and, of course, time travel. Unlike today's social networks, where information can be quickly disproved or verified, in the forums of the time, mysterious stories could germinate, grow and spread without too much interference.

The atmosphere of the forums: an almost underground space

It is important to understand that back then, the internet was not the ubiquitous juggernaut it is today. There was no Facebook or Twitter, and online communities were not connected in the way we now take for granted. Forums in the 2000s were like little secret groups, almost like underground societies where people could discuss theories and speculations that would not have been welcome in the "real" world. Anonymity offered a kind of protective shield for those who wanted to explore ideas that, outside these spaces, might have been dismissed as ridiculous or marginal.

In these forums, the etiquette was different: conversations were not necessarily brief, nor was there a race for "likes" or quick comments. It was a space where ideas were matured, discussed over time, and participants shared long texts explaining their views. It is in this environment that John Titor found an audience willing to listen and analyse, an audience that was not looking for immediate answers but for complex theories that could challenge their perception of the world.

The type of users frequenting these forums

The users who inhabited these forums were not just science fiction fans or dreamers. Many of them were highly educated, interested in science, technology and conspiracy theories, but there were also a large number of people dealing with the uncertainty of a changing world. The late 1990s and the beginning of the new millennium were complex times, with the rise of the internet, fear of technological failure, and a growing awareness of how digital advances could change the world in unpredictable ways.

This mix of the curious and the expert created an environment where topics that would have been ridiculed elsewhere - such as time travel - could be discussed with a degree of seriousness. Many of these people not only wanted to fantasise, but also to understand the limits of what was possible from a scientific perspective. For them, the forum offered a space where they could immerse themselves in the more extreme possibilities of science and technology.

The Time "Travel Institute" and the fascination with the impossible

Within this digital landscape, the **"Time Travel Institute"** occupied a special place. It was a forum devoted entirely to speculation about time travel, a subject that fascinated scientists and dreamers alike. Ever since

H.G. Wells popularised the concept of the time machine in his famous novel, the idea of moving through different epochs had captured the imagination of generations. But at the Time Travel Institute, this speculation was taken a step further. Here, not only were theories debated, but many of the participants genuinely believed in the possibility that time travel was real.

It is in this context that "*TimeTravel_0*" made its appearance. It was not received with great fanfare; after all, it was not uncommon for people claiming to be time travellers to emerge on that forum. But unlike other users, who simply spouted grandiose claims, "*TimeTravel_0*" began to construct a complex and detailed narrative. This is where the mystery began to take hold.

The visual language of the time

Although the forums of the time were primarily places for exchanging text, the visual aspect also played an important role in how the mystery was constructed. The avatars, custom signatures and banners that users added to their posts helped to create an atmosphere that reinforced the "secret" or "underground" character of these places. The simplicity of the designs, with dark backgrounds and low-resolution graphics, added a kind of rawness that made the conversations seem more clandestine. Forums of this type had an air of exclusivity, and this visual style helped to cement the idea that those who participated were part of something that others could not understand.

A discreet appearance that resonated deeply

At first, many ignored his postings. After all, stories about time travellers were nothing new on the forums. However, there was something different about "*TimeTravel_0*". He did not limit himself to the vague or fanciful claims that so many others made. Its tone was cold, detailed, almost military. It was not your typical science fiction story embellished with far-fetched fantasies, but a meticulous account that sounded more like a military operation than a fantasy adventure. He claimed to be an

American soldier from the year 2036, sent back in time with a specific mission: to retrieve an IBM 5100 computer from 1975, a device that, in his timeline, was crucial to avert a technological catastrophe.

This mission seemed so mundane and specific that, instead of generating disbelief, it began to attract the attention of forum users. Why would a simple computer from 1975 be so important for the future? This question was the hook that led many to follow his postings with increasing interest. The key to his success was not only the idea of time travel, but the way he presented it: coherent, detailed, and with impeccable internal logic.

A story with intriguing details

What really began to capture the attention of forum users was the level of detail he provided. From the beginning, his story was full of technicalities and explanations that, by the standards of the forums of the time, seemed strangely plausible. Why would anyone invent such a meticulous story, so full of data? Why mention a computer as specific as the IBM 5100, when many users at the time did not even know of its existence?

The fact that *TimeTravel_0*'s mission involved something so seemingly mundane - recovering a computer from the 1970s - gave it a layer of realism that few time-traveller stories have achieved before. He wasn't trying to save the world or stop some intergalactic cataclysm. His mission was precise, limited, and that made it all the more intriguing. It sounded more like a tale of military espionage than a simple fantasy. This set off a frenzy on the forums, where users began to investigate on their own, seeking more information about the IBM 5100 and corroborating whether what *2TimeTravel_0*" was saying could have any basis in reality.

The rise of technology as an underlying context

Importantly, all this happened at a time when technology was growing exponentially. The Internet was in its expansion phase, personal computers were becoming more common and accessible, and the dotcom bubble was booming. People were beginning to see the impact of technology on their daily lives, and with this technological growth also came many questions. Where was the world going? What implications would this new digital world have for humanity?

Titor's story appeared in a context where people were already struggling to understand the future of technology, and his tale struck a chord. He was talking about a computer from the past that would be vital to avert a disaster in the future. That combination of technology and inevitable destiny was extremely seductive to an audience already wrestling with similar questions about the future of humanity and the role of technology in that future.

The story of a traveller who knows his technology

As "*TimeTravel_0*" continued to post messages, it was the level of detail with which he described his world, the technology he used, and the time machine that had transported him into the past that really began to separate his story from other conspiracy theories and fantastical accounts circulating in the forums. According to his account, the time machine was powered by wormholes, generated by gravitational singularities. Such explanations not only seemed to be borrowed from emerging scientific theories, but also contained a level of accuracy that piqued the curiosity of even the most technologically savvy audience.

Throughout his posts, Titor painted a picture of his timeline: a future devastated by civil war in the United States, followed by a nuclear conflict in 2015 that would have left the world in a post-apocalyptic state. He described how life in his time had regressed to a more primitive style, with small self-sufficient communities and technologies reduced to the essential minimum. In this sense, his account spoke not only of a time machine, but of a hopeless future that, for many, resonated with the fears and anxieties of the time.

The art of time machine construction

One of the elements that had the greatest impact on Titor's credibility was his description of the time machine. Unlike the film versions full of futuristic lights and sounds, Titor described his time machine as something almost technical, a mechanical creation that seemed to have been conceived by engineers rather than science fiction writers. He spoke of gravitational singularities, of how extreme gravitational forces could create wormholes that would allow travel through time. This was not something the forums heard every day, let alone with that level of precision.

Interestingly, Titor's explanation of temporal technology resonated with some emerging theories in physics at the time. String theory and wormhole concepts had already begun to open debates in scientific circles. While most physicists felt that these concepts were still far from being applicable in the real world, Titor described them with the familiarity of someone who worked with them every day.

This technical language, which many forum members found incomprehensible, lent his account unexpected credibility. It didn't seem like the kind of story that someone would cobble together without serious research, and that raised a reasonable doubt among users: what if this man really knew something we didn't?

The rise of the conspiracy in the forums

At that time, theories about secret governments, occult societies and experiments with advanced technologies were an integral part of the forum culture. People not only discussed time travel, but also mind control, aliens and government conspiracies. Titor's story fit perfectly into this narrative, making it all the more credible to those who were already predisposed to accept that governments might be hiding advanced technologies.

The idea of a secret military division in charge of managing time travel, as Titor mentioned, did not seem at all far-fetched in that environment. For many, his story was simply a confirmation of their worst fears: that the government already had access to technologies unknown to the public, and that these technologies were being used for purposes they could not even imagine.

The construction of an interactive myth

What really made the difference with John Titor was his interaction with forum users. Unlike other science fiction stories or conspiracy theories that were posted and then disappeared, Titor was there, answering questions, offering more detail, adjusting his account as users questioned him. This created a sense of immediacy and authenticity that was hard to replicate.

Users were not just reading your story, they were participating in it. They were actively involved in the development of your story, which gave them a kind of ownership over the narrative. This not only amplified the spread of the story, but also made it harder to disprove or debunk. By interacting with users, Titor could clarify doubts, correct misunderstandings and add details that made his story seem even more realistic.

The story expands: from forum to forum

Gradually, John Titor's story began to move beyond the confines of the Time Travel Institute. Other online forums and communities began to pick up fragments of his story, and what was at first a small local curiosity became a wider phenomenon. Some users even began to create charts and timelines based on Titor's posts, trying to piece together all the pieces of the puzzle. Predictably, debates raged: sceptics tried to refute his claims, while others defended them, based on the consistency of his account and the apparent technological coincidences he mentioned.

What started as a simple forum thread became a narrative that spanned multiple online communities. The impact of the story was such that even those who were initially sceptical could not help but follow it. Users found themselves immersed in a cycle of speculation, with each new post by Titor generating more questions than answers.

The escalation of the Titor phenomenon on the internet

As more and more people began to follow John Titor's story, it spread beyond the Time Travel Institute, quickly spreading to other forums and corners of the internet. Users who were initially sceptical began to show a more serious curiosity: what if there really was some truth to what this man was saying? His consistency and the depth of his answers made his account difficult to dismiss completely.

The context in which Titor emerged was also crucial to its success. At the turn of the millennium, the world was facing radical changes in technology, geopolitics and culture. Fears of nuclear war, conspiracy theories about secret governments, and a sense that the future was out of control, made Titor's story resonate all the more strongly.

From simple user to digital myth

Eventually, the alias "*TimeTravel_0*" fell out of use, and was replaced by a name that would live on in the collective memory of the internet: John Titor. At that point, Titor went from being just another user on a forum to becoming an iconic figure in digital culture. His story was not only discussed in conspiracy or time travel forums, but began to appear in blogs, articles and, eventually, books. Titor had become a modern myth, a time traveller whose warning of a devastated future continued to resonate.

Philosophical and emotional implications of Titor's story

Another aspect that helped to expand the popularity of John Titor's story was the level of philosophical and emotional implications its messages conveyed. The idea of a devastated future and the possibility of changing the past to alter destiny resonated deeply with those who felt that the world was already on the brink of catastrophe. In the late 1990s and early 2000s, people were grappling with fears of globalisation, uncontrolled technological advances and the fragility of the economic system. In this context, Titor's warnings seemed not only plausible, but necessary to take into account.

Many users began to see Titor as more than just a time traveller. Some saw him as a kind of digital prophet, warning of the dangers that awaited us if we did not change the course of history. This message resonated deeply with a generation that had grown up in fear of the Cold War, nuclear meltdown and growing global uncertainty. Titor was not just talking about science and technology; he was touching the deepest fibres of human fear of the future.

The cultural impact of a temporary traveller

Finally, one of the greatest achievements of John Titor's story was how it became embedded in popular internet culture. For many, his story symbolised more than just a science fiction tale: it was a reflection on the limits of technology and the fate of humanity. As his story spread and branched out into multiple forums, it began to generate a cult-like following. He was seen not just as a prophet or a time traveller, but as a symbol of the uncertainty and mystery that surrounded the digital world in its early years.

The limits of scepticism at the time

Finally, one of the key factors in John Titor's success was the limited ability to verify information that existed at the time. Today, with advanced search engines, social networking and fact-checking sites, it is easier than ever to disprove extraordinary claims. But in the 2000s, the tools were rudimentary and rumours could circulate for much longer without being debunked. In many ways, the internet was like the Wild West: vast, unregulated, and full of opportunities for stories like Titor's to gain traction.

The difficulty in verifying his story, coupled with the growing interest in conspiracy theories and paranormal phenomena, helped Titor's tale spread before it could be completely disproven. This allowed time for his narrative to take hold in the collective psyche of the forums, resulting in a story that felt plausible for longer than it probably would have in current times.

2.2 Predictions and failures: What was right and what was wrong?

It is impossible to talk about John Titor without going into his predictions. While many people were hooked by his account of time travel, it was his ability to talk about future events that really captured the imagination of so many. After all, who wouldn't want to know what the future held? Predictions have always been a powerful hook, and in Titor's case, his claims were detailed enough to seem eerily real.

A US civil war that never came

Titor did not mince his words when talking about the future. One of his most shocking statements was the prediction of a civil war in the United States, which, according to his account, would begin in 2004. This war was not an ordinary political or social conflict, but a devastating confrontation between different factions within the country, caused by irreconcilable internal tensions. According to Titor, these tensions had built up due to a growing distrust of the government, the breakdown of civil liberties and the rise of mass surveillance, issues that, in his account, were already eroding social cohesion in the 2000s.

The war he described would not be quick or superficial. On the contrary, it represented the total fragmentation of the country into multiple warring factions, each with its own ideologies, interests and territories. The United States, in this future, would be divided into several independent regions, and the war would deeply affect the civilian population, disintegrating traditional governmental structures. The struggle for essential resources and control of the country's fundamental institutions would mark this war, which Titor described with almost frightening accuracy, making his prediction resonate with some sectors of the audience in this context.

To understand why this prediction had such an impact, it is crucial to remember the context of the early 2000s. The previous decade had been marked by prosperity, but also by growing paranoia and internal division. The 1995 Oklahoma City bombing, fears of domestic extremist and militia groups, and distrust of the government were creating an atmosphere of instability. But it was 11 September 2001 that really changed the perception of security in the country. New homeland security policies, such as the Patriot Act, and increased communications surveillance were perceived by some as an attack on civil liberties, exactly the concerns that Titor claimed would trigger civil war.

At the political level, the divisions between ideologies were palpable, with increasing confrontation over issues such as civil rights, privacy, and the scope of government powers. Mistrust of public institutions and growing political polarisation created a breeding ground that, for some, made Titor's vision seem not so far-fetched. Moreover, many recalled episodes of domestic violence and how political fragmentation had already been present in US history during the Civil War of 1861. The possibility that the country might once again be divided did not seem so unlikely in the minds of those who feared that the events of the turn of the millennium were a prelude to something worse.

Most worryingly, according to Titor, the civil war that erupted in 2004 would not only fragment the United States, but would escalate until 2015, when it would culminate in a global nuclear conflict. In his version of the future, international tensions and local conflicts would eventually trigger a nuclear confrontation that would plunge the entire world into chaos. The survivors would be forced to rebuild from scratch, and the United States would be divided into five independent regions, each trying to survive amidst the wreckage of civilisation.

Yet here we are in 2024, and none of this has happened as he described it. There was no open civil war in 2004, no global nuclear conflict in 2015 that left the planet devastated. This is one of the most criticised and debated points by those who are sceptical of John Titor's story: how could someone from the future fail to predict something so great, something that, had it happened, would have irreversibly shaped human history?

Titor's defenders have argued that the absence of these events can be explained through the theory of divergent timelines that he himself mentioned. According to this theory, the simple fact that Titor travelled into the past and shared his story with people could have created a new timeline in which these events did not happen as he predicted. That is, Titor's actions in our timeline could have altered the course of events, preventing or delaying the civil war and nuclear conflict he described. This explanation, while convenient for some, does not convince everyone and remains the subject of debate between those who believe in the authenticity of his account and those who consider it a myth.

The lack of a civil war in the timeframe described, coupled with the absence of a global nuclear conflict in 2015, has been one of the main points that sceptics have used to discredit Titor's story. However, others point out that political and social tensions in the United States, especially since the polarisation of the last decade, could still be interpreted as indications that, while armed conflict did not materialise on the dates indicated, the foundations of distrust and deep division in US society are more present than ever. For some, the polarised elections, political radicalisation and recent civil unrest could be interpreted as the first symptoms of what Titor predicted, even if the outcome has taken a different direction in our timeline.

Ultimately, Titor's prediction of a US civil war that never came raises more questions than it answers, and his failure to anticipate such a major event remains one of the major criticisms of his story. Even so, the ideas he presented about social fragmentation and the erosion of freedoms remain relevant themes, allowing his account to continue to fuel imagination and speculation in forums, books and debates about what might have been.

The divergent timelines factor

John Titor's defenders, however, did not give up so easily on these failures in his predictions. One theory that gained popularity was the idea that Titor himself had warned of **divergent timelines**. According to this explanation, Titor did not travel into the past of his own timeline, but, in doing so, created a new, alternate reality. Thus, the events he described - including civil war and nuclear conflict - did occur in his original timeline, but his interaction with our past altered the course of events, preventing (or delaying) these catastrophes in our timeline.

This notion of divergent timelines rested on the idea that every decision, every change, creates a new branch of reality, and this was one way of explaining why Titor's predictions did not materialise in our timeline. For some, this was enough to hold out hope that Titor had been genuine. For others, it only served as a convenient excuse to justify the errors in his predictions.

Technological advances: surprising successes and shadows of doubt

Major political events aside, one of the most interesting aspects of Titor's predictions was his knowledge of technology. Indeed, some of his comments on technological advances surprised many, and while not all of his predictions were accurate, several technical details turned out to be surprisingly precise, giving his story an unexpected amount of credibility.

One of the most fascinating examples of his technological predictions was his mention of the **IBM 5100**, a computer he claimed he needed to bring back from 1975 because of a special capability it possessed: the emulation of certain programming languages. Titor explained that the IBM 5100 had a functionality that was not known to the general public, but that it would be crucial in his future timeline to solve a problem related to **Unix** systems that could cause disastrous consequences if not addressed. This flaw, which he described as a kind of **technological time bomb**, put at risk vital computer systems in his society and required the intervention of a computer that could interface with older systems, such as the IBM 5100.

What is more intriguing is that, at the time Titor made this claim, the hidden ability of the IBM 5100 to emulate programming languages such as **APL** and **BASIC** was not a publicly known fact. This functionality was known only to a small group of engineers who had worked directly on its development. In fact, this capability allowed large corporations and some government sectors to avoid system incompatibility problems, making it a crucial tool for certain specialised projects. The subsequent revelation by engineers who had worked on the development of the IBM 5100 confirming the existence of this hidden capability caused many to reconsider Titor's story. For some, it was hard to imagine how someone without privileged access to such information could have known about it, leading to speculation as to whether he really could have been a time traveller or someone with highly advanced technical connections.

Titor's fear of a failure of Unix systems and their relationship to this computer touched a sensitive nerve at the time, as the years leading up to the turn of the millennium had seen the **Y2K** scare, which generated panic about the potential failure of older computer systems at the turn of the millennium. Although the Y2K problem turned out not to be as devastating as some predicted, Titor's prediction resonated with those same anxieties about the fragility of technological infrastructure and the danger of relying on older systems unprepared for certain changes. This level of technical detail made his claims about technology harder for some to dismiss than his more grandiose political predictions.

In addition to the IBM 5100, Titor also made other technological predictions that, while not fully realised, touched on issues that are still debated today. He spoke of advances in **quantum physics** and the use of **wormholes** and **gravitational singularities** to facilitate time travel. While these ideas were not entirely new to the scientific world or science fiction, the way he described them suggested advanced technical knowledge that, to some, sounded plausible in the framework of speculative physical theories.

For example, Titor mentioned that his time machine was equipped with twin singularities that generated gravitational fields powerful enough to distort space-time and allow time travel. Although science has not yet proven that these concepts can be applied to time travel, wormholes and gravitational singularities are topics that continue to be studied in the field of theoretical physics. The detailed descriptions he offered of the **physical principles behind his time machine** caused some science-literate followers to speculate whether Titor was somehow connected to scientific advances beyond what was publicly accessible at the time.

Another technological prediction Titor made was the **development of decentralised systems**, something that today could be linked to the rise of technologies such as **blockchain** and cryptocurrencies. Although he did not specifically mention these innovations, he spoke of a growing distrust of centralised institutions and how the technology of the future would allow for greater independence from traditional government and financial systems. The idea of a decentralised network in which individuals could interact directly without intermediaries seemed an early reflection of the technological movements that emerged in the following decades, when control over data and finance became a central theme in the discussion about the future of technology.

Titor also suggested that in the future there would be a greater reliance on local technologies and **technological self-sufficiency**. This was reflected in his predictions of a future in which large cities would be abandoned and communities would live in small self-sufficient settlements, where technology would not be completely absent, but would be limited and locally controlled. While this post-apocalyptic vision has not come to pass, there are elements of his prediction that resonate today with modern movements such as **"tech minimalism"** and the increasing reliance on renewable energy and local solutions to global problems such as climate change.

In short, although many of Titor's technological predictions have not been fully realised, some of his comments have found echoes in modern technological discussions. His accuracy about the IBM 5100 remains one of the most striking details of his story, while his comments about gravitational singularities, decentralised networks and the growing distrust of centralised systems remain topics of discussion in today's world. For some, Titor's prediction about the future of technology was more a warning about our growing dependence on systems that, if not carefully managed, could collapse under their own weight.

Quantum physics and advanced scientific theories

One of the most striking points about John Titor's predictions was his knowledge of advanced scientific concepts related to **quantum physics** and the possibility of time travel. What made his account so intriguing to some was the way he talked about phenomena that were already being studied by theoretical physicists at the time, but had not yet been demonstrated or fully understood.

Titor mentioned **wormholes** and **gravitational singularities** as the basis of his time machine, explaining that, through these spatial anomalies, it was possible to distort space-time and travel back in time. Although science has not yet found a practical way to manipulate these phenomena, the idea of wormholes was not new to theoretical physics, but his technical precision in describing them caused surprise in certain circles.

The concept of wormholes, also known as **Einstein-Rosen bridges**, comes from Einstein's theory of general relativity. According to this theory, wormholes are shortcuts in the fabric of space-time that could, in theory, connect two distant points in space and time. Speculation about whether wormholes could be used for time travel has been a popular topic in science fiction and scientific theory since the mid-20th century. Titor claimed that his time machine used twin **gravitational singularities** to generate these wormholes, creating extremely powerful gravitational fields capable of bending space-time.

What makes his explanation interesting is that, although it sounds like science fiction, wormholes and gravitational singularities are real topics of study in theoretical physics. Physicists have speculated that, under certain extreme conditions, such as the manipulation of **negative energy** or **exotic matter**, it might be possible to stabilise a wormhole enough to serve as a temporary bridge. However, to date, this remains purely theoretical, as creating and manipulating wormholes in real life would be incredibly difficult and would require immense energy levels.

The **gravitational singularity**, which is also a recurring theme in black hole theory, refers to a point in space where the laws of physics as we know them no longer apply. Black holes are examples of regions of space where singularities exist, and within their "event horizon" gravity is so strong that nothing, not even light, can escape. In Titor's theory, his time machine used two controlled gravitational singularities to generate a field capable of creating a stable wormhole. This allowed him to travel through time without being destroyed by extreme gravitational forces, something that science has not yet been able to prove or reproduce.

What also surprised many was how Titor connected these concepts to the laws of **quantum mechanics**, a branch of physics that describes phenomena on extremely small scales, such as subatomic particles. In previous decades, quantum mechanics had already shown that particles can exist in superposition states, meaning that they can be in more than one place at the same time. Moreover, the famous phenomenon of **quantum entanglement** suggested that particles could interact instantaneously across vast distances, something Albert Einstein once described as ghostly action at a distance. Titor did not mention quantum entanglement specifically, but his claims about using gravitational singularities to manipulate time seemed to be based on an advanced understanding of quantum principles.

Although these ideas have yet to be tested on a practical level, the fact that Titor discussed them in such detail made some scientists and technology enthusiasts intrigued by the possibility that he was actually describing a plausible theoretical model. While many of his claims may have been an extension of the speculative science of the time, some argue that his description of physical phenomena was sufficiently advanced to make it difficult to dismiss as mere invention.

Another concept Titor mentioned in his messages was the idea that **the timeline could be altered**, a key point in his explanations of how time travel did not affect his original future, but created a **new timeline**. This idea is closely related to the quantum interpretation of the multiverse, which holds that there are multiple realities or parallel universes. According to this theory, every decision or event can create a new timeline, and time travellers, such as Titor, would not necessarily affect their own future, but simply enter a new parallel reality. This theory remains a hotly debated topic in modern physics, particularly in the field of quantum cosmology, where the possibility of multiple universes existing simultaneously is explored.

Furthermore, Titor mentioned that the effects of time travel were **controlled and monitored** by a military division at the time. He claimed that time travel technology was not available to everyone, but was a tool controlled by a government elite, a claim that struck at the heart of conspiracy theories that already existed at the time about government control of advanced science. At a time when technology and physics were advancing rapidly, Titor's predictions of military use of advanced technologies to alter time seemed at least theoretically possible.

Of course, much of what Titor described in relation to quantum physics and time travel remains speculative, but the connections between his account and theoretical developments in physics gave him a technical credibility that few expected. Although no practical advances have been made in the field of time travel through gravitational singularities or wormholes, science continues to explore these concepts in search of answers. Discoveries in theoretical physics, from the **Higgs boson** to **gravitons**, suggest that there is still much we do not know about the universe, and the ideas Titor put forward continue to fascinate scientists and science fiction enthusiasts alike.

In short, although it has not been proven that wormholes or gravitational singularities can be used for time travel, the theories Titor mentioned followed plausible scientific paths at the time and continue to be studied today. For some, it was the fact that Titor was able to speak so clearly about these concepts that gave his story an air of authenticity, while for others it is no more than an extrapolation of the speculative science that already existed. Nevertheless, the impact of his claims continues to fuel imagination and debates about the future of physics and technology.

Fading predictions: Missed opportunities?

While many of his predictions about technology were echoed in reality or at least connected to plausible theories, it is also true that some of his broader and more general statements simply did not materialise. Titor spoke of breakthroughs that would allow humans to master time travel and space-time manipulation with gravitational singularities, something that remains a topic of debate in modern science, but which we have not seen realised in practice.

Moreover, his warnings about social collapse and emerging technology seemed tailor-made for millennium fears. However, the world has not collapsed as he described it, and although political and social tensions have grown, we have not seen conflict on the scale he predicted.

The role of the media

The **impact of the media** was crucial in turning the John Titor myth from a story confined to internet forums into a global phenomenon. While the original narrative developed in niche communities, its reach grew exponentially thanks to **radio shows**, **digital news**, and **mass media** that began to address time travel, future mysteries, and government conspiracies.

Popular programmes such as **"Coast to Coast AM"**, famous for its audience interested in the paranormal and conspiracy theories, began inviting experts and discussing John Titor's authenticity. This kind of media coverage was instrumental in getting more people to learn about his story and join the debate. Some digital media exploring paranormal topics also began to write about him, which broadened his exposure.

The **rise of the internet** as an information platform was key to this phenomenon. In the early 2000s, information flowed rapidly through websites, mailing lists and online communities. Traditional media, in turn, saw Titor's story as a way to connect with an audience increasingly intrigued by what the internet had to offer. Indeed, **articles in tech media and science forums** began to analyse Titor's predictions more seriously, breaking down their technological and social implications.

This not only kept the myth of John Titor alive, but also **legitimised his story** in certain quarters, as some media outlets and programmes spent hours analysing the possible truths behind his claims. Today, John Titor continues to be a subject of documentaries, books and even video games exploring time travel and government conspiracies.

Secret military technology

One of the most fascinating points of John Titor's story was his claim that **time travel was not just a scientific breakthrough, but a technology controlled by the military**. According to him, he worked for a secret military division in charge of managing time travel, suggesting that this technology was seen as a strategic advantage in their timeline.

This aspect of his story connected to some of the **most entrenched conspiracy theories** in popular culture. The idea that governments are

hiding technological advances that could change the course of history is not new. From theories about **advanced weapons** to ideas about the **manipulation of time** as a weapon of war, the notion that the military has access to technologies unknown to the general population has always been a source of speculation.

Historically, there have been numerous cases of **secret military technology** being revealed to the public. Examples such as the **Manhattan Project**, the development of nuclear weapons during World War II, and the creation of the **internet** as an early military project are examples of how governments have hidden and used advanced technologies for years before making them public. These later revelations help to make John Titor's narrative more credible to some, as the possibility of time-controlled technologies in the hands of a secret military elite does not seem so far-fetched to those who believe in such theories.

Trivial but intriguing predictions

Titor not only made predictions about major events such as civil wars and nuclear conflicts, but also a number of smaller, seemingly trivial predictions that, while less dramatic, are equally intriguing. Some of these smaller predictions offer insights into the changes in everyday life following the global collapse he described, and many of them seem to connect to current concerns about sustainability and the future of resources.

One of the most interesting predictions was the assertion that, following the collapse of major political and economic systems, the **use of motorised vehicles would become much more limited** due to **fuel shortages**. Titor argued that the global collapse would result in a severe energy crisis, leading to a drastic change in the way people travel. According to his account, **bicycle travel** and the **use of horses** would become much more common, while motorised vehicles, which relied on fossil fuels, would be virtually reserved for situations of extreme need or for those with access to privileged resources.

While this prediction may seem irrelevant compared to his other claims, it reflects very real concerns that already existed in the 2000s, especially related to the **scarcity of energy resources** and the environmental impact of the world's dependence on oil. At that time, there was already a growing debate about **peak oil**, the theory that world oil production would peak and then begin to decline, causing a global energy crisis. Although so far we have not witnessed a total collapse of energy resources, concerns about sustainability and the search for **alternative energy sources** have increased enormously in recent decades.

A modern parallel to his prediction can be seen in the increased use of **bicycles** and **electric vehicles** in response to the climate crisis and the need to reduce carbon emissions. Cities around the world have begun to adopt infrastructures that promote more sustainable modes of transport, such as bike lanes and public bike rental systems. In addition, the rise of **electric vehicles** has been an attempt to mitigate the impact of fossil fuels on the environment. While we have not seen a total reliance on bicycles and horses as Titor predicted, the transition to more sustainable modes of transport is a current reality that resonates with his predictions.

In addition to the change in transport, Titor also predicted that society in general would become more **self-reliant** after the collapse of large governmental and economic systems. According to him, resource scarcity would force people to rely less on centralised infrastructures and more on local solutions for survival. This would include the creation of **small, self-sufficient communities**, where technology would still exist, but in a limited and locally controlled way. Solar, wind and other renewable resources would become the main source of energy, as fossil fuels would become scarce or inaccessible.

Although this prediction of total collapse has not occurred, the movement towards **local sustainability** and **self-sufficiency** has grown considerably in recent decades. Around the world, movements have sprung up for the creation of **ecovillages** and **self-sustainable communities**, where people grow their own food, produce their own energy and reduce their carbon footprint. The rise of solar and wind energy as an alternative to fossil fuels is also closely aligned with Titor's vision of a society that relies on more sustainable technologies. These movements, while not emerging as a result of catastrophic collapse, reflect a growing concern about the limits of industrial growth and the impact of massive resource consumption on the planet.

Another minor but intriguing prediction by Titor concerned **education**. According to him, after the social collapse, the education system would be drastically transformed. Centralised schools would disappear and be replaced by a system in which **knowledge was shared in a more local** and practical **way. Teachers would be respected individuals** within communities, and education would focus more on the skills needed for survival and the development of local technology, rather than on abstract subjects. Titor argued that, in his time, a focus on practical skills and self-reliance was key to survival in a devastated world.

While we have not seen the total collapse of the traditional education system, the **digital revolution** in education has brought profound changes in the way people learn. The rise of **online learning**, **digital educational platforms** and **self-education** through resources accessible on the internet reflects, in a sense, Titor's vision of decentralised education. Today, millions of people have access to platforms such as **Khan Academy**, **Coursera** and **edX**, where they can learn everything from programming to agriculture without having to attend a centralised educational institution. In addition, the recent COVID-19 pandemic accelerated the transition to more **flexible** education models tailored to local and personal needs, another reflection of the change Titor hinted at in his dystopian future.

Another interesting prediction Titor mentioned was the **decline of big cities**. According to his version of the future, large cities would be abandoned or drastically reduced in population, as access to resources and the danger of armed conflict would lead people to prefer to live in **smaller rural communities**. Although this prediction has not been fully realised, we have seen a **growing interest in rural living** and decentralisation in some sectors of society, especially after disruptive events such as the 2020 pandemic caused many people to reconsider their urban lifestyles. **Telecommuting** and **migration to rural areas** became growing trends during and after the pandemic, which, while not a direct reflection of a catastrophic collapse, does touch on some of Titor's ideas about how societies would restructure the way they live.

In short, although many of Titor's trivial predictions have not materialised in exactly the way he described, many of his ideas about **self-sufficiency**, **sustainability** and **changes in education and transport** have found resonance in the modern world. In a sense, his predictions seem to reflect some of the most pressing contemporary concerns, such as the energy crisis, climate change and the quest for more sustainable lifestyles.

2.3 Theories about his identity: A military man, a prankster or a marketing genius?

The figure of John Titor has not only generated debates about time travel, but has also given rise to countless theories about who he really was. Over the years, hypotheses about his identity and motivations have multiplied. Some of these theories seem plausible, while others border on the more fantastic speculation: was he really a soldier from the future sent on a mission, or just someone with too much time on his hands and a big imagination? This is one of the great unknowns that have kept John Titor's story alive for more than two decades.

One of the simplest but most plausible theories is that John Titor was an **exceptionally skilled prankster**. According to this hypothesis, Titor was merely an individual with an advanced knowledge of technology and physics, who decided to create a fascinating narrative and let the online community in on it. This type of hoax is not new to the internet, but the level of detail and consistency in his posts makes this theory not so easy to accept. Supporters argue that Titor, with great creativity and technical skills, would have woven a story convincing enough to capture the attention of forum users, who then expanded and perpetuated the myth. Moreover, the fact that Titor's narrative has been kept alive for so many years suggests that, if it was a hoax, it was incredibly well executed.

Despite this, some argue that Titor**'s level of technical and scientific detail**, especially regarding the IBM 5100 and its ability to emulate certain programming languages, was too advanced to have been simply the result of a joke. This information was not public knowledge at the time, which makes it difficult to believe that someone without access to privileged information could have known about it. Moreover, the fact that Titor's account was so consistent throughout his multiple publications is also a point that makes sceptics doubt that it was simply a hoax.

Another intriguing theory that has emerged over the years is that John Titor was part of a **government experiment**, perhaps related to disinformation or even mass psychological manipulation. This idea fits well with the paranoia surrounding **secret government experiments** in the 2000s, when Titor's story began to spread. From Project MKUltra to rumours about Area 51, government experiments in espionage, mind control and advanced technology have been a constant source of conspiracy theories.

According to this hypothesis, Titor may have been part of a **military or government experiment** designed to see how the public would react to the idea of time travel. This also relates to the fact that Titor claimed to work for a secret military division in the future, charged with managing and controlling time travel. Proponents of this theory argue that, if he really was part of a disinformation experiment, his story and the reactions it provoked could have been used to analyse how people would react to the notion that the government has access to advanced technologies that have not been made public. This "social proof" approach would fit the style of certain psychological and sociological experiments conducted in the past by governments around the world.

However, perhaps one of the most fascinating theories is that John Titor was part of a **viral marketing campaign**. In the early 2000s, the concept of **viral marketing** was beginning to take hold, and some speculate that Titor's story was actually an attempt to promote a product, be it a book, a movie, or even a video game. Titor's narrative, with its mix of science fiction, military intrigue and speculation about the future, seemed to fit perfectly with the kind of guerrilla marketing that was beginning to be experimented with at the time. In fact, early attempts at viral campaigns often used enigmatic characters or stories to generate interest and conversation, before revealing the product being promoted.

The curious thing about this theory is that, while plausible, the product or project that was supposedly behind the campaign has never come to light. This has only fuelled further speculation, with many wondering: if it really was a marketing ploy, why was nothing associated with John Titor's story ever released? Some suggest that the campaign may have failed or been cancelled, leaving the story without a clear conclusion, which would explain why the purpose behind its creation was never revealed. Others speculate that perhaps the Titor story grew beyond what the original creators expected, becoming an independent and uncontrolled phenomenon, which would have made it impossible to follow through with the original marketing plan.

Finally, there is the most fantastic possibility of all, but also the one that has captured the imagination of many: that John Titor **really was a time traveller**. According to this theory, Titor was a soldier sent from the year 2036 on a mission to save his timeline from technological catastrophe. This theory remains a favourite among those who believe in the possibility of time travel and conspiracy stories involving advanced technologies hidden by the government. If this theory were true, then

Titor would come from a different timeline than ours, which would explain why some of his predictions did not come true in our reality.

This idea is based on the theory of **divergent timelines**, which Titor mentioned in his publications. According to this theory, every time someone travels into the past, he does not change his own future, but creates a new alternative timeline. Thus, the events in his original timeline would have occurred as he described them (such as the civil war in the United States or the global nuclear conflict), but by interacting with our past, he created a deviation, which led to those events not manifesting in the same way in our reality. Although this theory is highly speculative and lacks evidence, it remains the most attractive to those who wish to believe in the possibility of time travel.

In short, John Titor's identity remains a mystery. From a witty prankster, to a pawn in a government experiment, or even a genuine time traveller, theories about who he really was have kept his story alive for more than 20 years. While Titor's story continues to fuel debate and speculation, one thing is certain: his legend has left an indelible mark on modern digital culture.

Chapter 3: Andrew Basiago and Project Pegasus

If conspiracy theories were ranked by their level of audacity, Andrew Basiago's story would occupy a very special place. In a world where conspiracies range from UFO sightings to mind control experiments, Basiago's claims stand out not only for their content, but for their depth, the amount of detail he presents and the breadth of the events he allegedly experienced. In his account, time travel and teleportation are not just the stuff of science fiction, but operational technologies within top-secret US government programmes, all linked to a mysterious project called "Pegasus."

What makes Basiago's story so intriguing? For a start, he is no ordinary individual who simply turned up proclaiming that he had been abducted or had visions of the future. Andrew Basiago is a lawyer with respectable credentials and a political activist who ran for President of the United States. However, throughout his life, he has vehemently claimed that, when he was just a child, he was selected to participate in a top-secret US government experiment. This project, known as Project Pegasus, supposedly explored advanced technologies that defy the laws of physics as we know them: teleportation and time travel.

What really captures the attention about Basiago's claims is how he places his narrative in the context of the Cold War and the technological paranoia of that era. The 1960s and 1970s were decades marked by rapid advances in the space race, defence programmes and espionage technology, all amid fierce competition with the Soviet Union. In this climate of secrecy and mistrust, governments were willing to invest in crazy-sounding research in the hope of gaining some advantage over their enemies. From the Manhattan Project, which resulted in the creation of the atomic bomb, to the MKUltra mind-control experiments, governments, especially the United States, had already shown a predisposition to fund highly experimental and ethically questionable projects.

But Basiago's claims go far beyond simple scientific experiments. According to him, Project Pegasus was an initiative backed by DARPA (Defence Advanced Research Projects Agency), the same organisation that has been behind some of the most important technological advances of the 20th century, including the first prototypes of what we know today as the internet. According to Basiago, the goal of Project Pegasus was not simply to explore time and space out of scientific curiosity, but to use teleportation and time travel as tools to influence historical and strategic events. Imagine, for a moment, if the government had the ability not just to observe the past, but to influence it. How different would key decisions in recent history be if they were guided by people with the ability to jump through time?

Basiago claims that he was one of the many children selected to take part in this experiment, which adds an even more chilling dimension to his story. Why children? According to him, youth offered certain advantages in these experiments, such as greater physical and mental adaptability to temporal and spatial distortions. If this is true, it leads us to reflect on the morality of using children as subjects in such radical experiments, a question that immediately recalls the terrible experimental projects of the past, such as those that occurred during the Second World War.

But that is not the end of the mystery. Over the years, Basiago has offered detailed descriptions of his alleged travels, not only to key moments in US history, but also to places outside this planet. One of the most extraordinary aspects of his account is his claim to have been teleported to the planet Mars. At this point, Basiago's story not only challenges our understanding of time, but also of space, and forces us to wonder how far the capacity for technological manipulation goes if what he describes were remotely possible.

This is the kind of claim that generates both scepticism and fascination. What evidence does Basiago have to support his claims? In many cases, he has only his testimony. However, he has detailed several specific events, such as witnessing Abraham Lincoln's famous Gettysburg Address, and claims that evidence of his travels exists, albeit buried deep in secret government archives.

What makes his account more compelling to some is the web of conspiracy theories surrounding DARPA and other government research projects. During the Cold War, the US government funded experiments such as Project Stargate, actual research into psychic abilities, including remote viewing. This begs the question: if governments have been able to fund and execute such eccentric projects in the past, why wouldn't they be behind a teleportation and time travel programme?

From a philosophical point of view, Basiago's story also opens up a fascinating debate about the ethics and implications of manipulating time. If, hypothetically, we had the technology to travel through time, what would that mean for our understanding of free will? Would we have the ability to change the past or are we destined to follow timelines that have already been predetermined? This dilemma has been explored in science fiction time and time again, but in Basiago's narrative, it becomes a tangible possibility, an unsolved mystery.

Then there is the question of teleportation, a concept that seems to be a leap of the imagination, but actually has theoretical foundations in quantum physics. Although quantum teleportation has been demonstrated in experiments at the subatomic level, we are light years away from moving humans through space with this technology. However, Basiago claims that the government has already overcome these obstacles, using advanced technology that is kept hidden from the general public.

If what Andrew Basiago tells is true, this would completely change our understanding not only of time and space, but also of the very nature of reality. Could the government have access to technologies that defy our laws of physics, keeping them secret while we continue to live in a world with apparent technological limitations?

Basiago's story continues to spark debate, both among his defenders and his detractors. Some see him as a visionary, a pioneer who is revealing the deepest secrets of a government that hides the truth from us. Others see him as a fabulist, a man with an overflowing imagination who has built a science fiction narrative around his own life. What is undeniable is that Basiago's story, whether true or false, offers a window into the depths of our hopes, fears and speculations about what the future may hold.

Throughout this chapter, we will explore the most shocking details of their stories, but before we dive into the more extraordinary implications of their history, it is worth reflecting on an idea that has captivated humanity since time immemorial: what if all this were true? What would we do if we knew that everything we take for granted about time, space and history has been manipulated by a group of people who have the power to change everything?

3.1 Journeys to Mars, the Civil War and beyond

Andrew Basiago, a lawyer and political activist, has claimed over the years that he was a participant in a top-secret programme known as Project Pegasus, an initiative run by DARPA, the US Defence Advanced Research Projects Agency. What makes his statements among the most shocking in the world of conspiracy theories is the magnitude of what his account suggests. According to Basiago, this project involved not only unprecedented technological advances, but also the possibility of time travel and teleportation to other planets. From a young age, Basiago was reportedly selected to participate in these missions, and his experiences encompass a series of events that not only defy the laws of physics, but also our understanding of history and reality itself.

One of the most surprising elements of his account is the alleged trip to **Mars**. According to Basiago, he was teleported to the red planet on several occasions as part of exploration missions in which he was not alone. Other young people, also selected for Project Pegasus, were allegedly sent with him on these missions, and the reason the government chose children and teenagers, according to Basiago, was because of their ability to adapt better to the physical and psychological effects of teleportation. This is where the truly extraordinary begins: Basiago argues that Mars is not an uninhabited planet as we have been led to believe, but actually harbours extraterrestrial life.

According to him, the beings that inhabit Mars are not exactly like humans, but they possess some characteristics that make them similar to us. Basiago describes the inhabitants of Mars as **humanoid beings**, although different in many ways. Not all Mars missions, according to him, were peaceful. Some expeditions included **confrontations with Martian entities**, suggesting that not all Martians were receptive to human contact. Basiago also mentions that the most technologically advanced beings on Mars had developed **underground systems** to protect themselves from the hostile environment of the planet's surface, allowing them to live more safely. This detail suggests that Mars was not just a lifeless desert terrain, but possessed **an advanced society** hidden from human view.

In addition, Basiago reports that, in order to survive on Mars, the humans sent there were given **special equipment** that enabled them to withstand the Martian atmosphere and harsh weather conditions. This advanced technology reinforces the idea that the US government already had access to technological capabilities beyond what is revealed to the public. All of this raises questions about the true nature of life on Mars and what knowledge the authorities might be hiding.

As for the **teleportation technology** used to perform these journeys, Basiago gives a detailed description of how it worked. According to him, the teleportation in Project Pegasus was an incredibly advanced technology, which allowed participants to **jump** from one place to another on Earth, and even travel through space, reaching Mars. This technology, according to his account, worked similarly to a device that **broke down the human body into subatomic particles**, which were sent to their destination and then reassembled. While this process was **instantaneous**, it was also extremely **risky**. An error in the calibration of the teleportation equipment could completely disintegrate the traveller during the journey. Despite these risks, Basiago claims that the technology was sufficiently advanced to allow missions to Mars to occur on a regular basis, which raises a big question as to why this kind of technology is still hidden from the public if it was operational decades ago.

However, travel to Mars is only one part of Basiago's incredible story. According to him, Project Pegasus also explored the possibility of **time travel**, which adds another, even more fascinating dimension to his narrative. Basiago claims that he was sent to **pivotal moments** in US history, including such important events as the **American Civil War**. One of the most notable moments he claims to have been present at was **Abraham Lincoln's Gettysburg Address** in 1863. Basiago relates that he was teleported several times to this specific event, where he was able to observe first-hand one of the most iconic moments in American history.

Most intriguingly, Basiago insists that his role within Project Pegasus was that of an **observer**, someone who could not alter the course of historical events, but who was tasked with witnessing these moments in order to **study their unfolding**. This suggests that the government, at least at this stage of the project, was not interested in changing the past, but in learning from it in a more direct way than scholars might imagine. Still, the **mere presence** of a time traveller at such a critical event raises the possibility that, however inadvertently, his presence alone could alter the course of events.

In addition to the Civil War, Basiago also mentions being sent to **other key historical periods**. His accounts range from **classical antiquity** to significant moments in the **20th century**, and on some of these trips, he suggests that he was not alone, but part of a team. The purpose of this team was to observe and record events for future government research. This notion raises philosophical questions about the **ethical use** of time travel technology. If it really were possible to travel into the past without altering events, should the government have exclusive access to this information? What implications does this have for our understanding of history as we know it?

Basiago explains that the **historical context** in which these time travels took place was particularly relevant. According to him, the US government, especially during the **Cold War**, was obsessed with the idea of **monitoring not only the present, but also the past**. Major historical events, such as the Civil War or **World War II**, were monitored in the hope of finding patterns or information that could be used to **prevent future crises** or **anticipate global threats**. Project Pegasus would have allowed the government not only to learn from the past, but to use that knowledge to gain a **strategic advantage** over its rivals. This militaristic approach reinforces the idea that time travel was not just a scientific experiment, but part of a broader national security strategy.

In addition to these time missions, Basiago has mentioned the existence of **parallel realities**. According to him, some of the missions not only took him to different points in time within our timeline, but also to **alternate versions** of history, where events unfolded differently. This suggests that Project Pegasus was investigating the possibility of **multiple universes** or **timelines** coexisting simultaneously, and that events in one reality could influence events in another. Basiago suggests that every major decision we make in our lives has the potential to create a new timeline where events unfold differently. For example, in one of these alternate realities, the **United States would never have won the Civil War**, or **World War II** would have had a completely different outcome.

The **impact of these parallel realities** on our own timeline, according to Basiago, was one of the most intriguing aspects of Project Pegasus. He claims that the government was interested in studying how changes in these realities could affect the unfolding of our own history. This notion adds an even more complex layer to the story, suggesting that the decisions we make in our reality may be **affecting** not only our own future, but also the future of **other parallel realities**. If true, the implications for **physics** and **philosophy** are enormous, as it suggests that history is not a fixed path, but a **web of interconnected possibilities**.

One of the darker aspects of Basiago's account concerns the **lost time travellers**. Although many Project Pegasus missions were successful, according to Basiago, not all participants made it back. Some of the time travellers mysteriously disappeared and were never heard from again. According to Basiago, some of these travellers may have been trapped in **time loops**, where the same events are repeated over and over again with no chance of escape. Others, he says, may have been sent to **parallel realities** or points in time from which they could never return. These disappearances add a **tragic dimension** to the story, as the human cost of the project was far greater than has been revealed.

In addition to the physical danger, Basiago has spoken of the **psychological impact** these trips had on the participants, especially the children. According to him, children who participated in Project Pegasus suffered from **temporary disorientation** after the trips, resulting in a loss of awareness of where or when they were. After returning to their original time, some experienced severe **psychological side effects**, such as **recurring nightmares**, **memory loss** and even **hallucinations**. These symptoms, according to Basiago, were the result of the extreme stress caused by the jumps in time and space. In some cases, participants were subjected to **deprogramming** therapies, designed to **erase** memories of the missions and protect the confidentiality of the project. This raises **serious ethical questions** about the use of children in such dangerous experiments, and whether the government was really aware of the **traumatic effects** these journeys would have on the minds of young people.

As disturbing as Basiago's account may seem, his statements have generated **enormous interest** in both the conspiracy community and society at large. If what he claims is true, then Project Pegasus is one of the US government's best-kept secrets, a programme that not only challenges our understanding of **science** and **technology**, but also of **history**, **time** and **reality** itself. The implications of these claims are hard to ignore. If the government has been experimenting with technologies that enable time travel and teleportation, what other **advances** have they made, and why does the public still not know these details, if we have already travelled to Mars and explored the past?

Andrew Basiago's story is undoubtedly one of the most fascinating in the vast world of conspiracy theories. As more people begin to take an interest in his stories, the questions he raises about the nature of time, space and history continue to resonate. Whether his claims are truth or fiction, his account has left an **indelible** mark on popular culture and on the imaginations of those seeking answers about what really goes on behind the walls of the **most secretive government projects**.

3.2 Government conspiracy or pure fantasy?

As Andrew Basiago continued to tell his story to the world, more people began to wonder: could there be any truth to his claims, or is it simply a well-crafted fantasy? His tales of time travel, teleportation and secret missions to Mars have inevitably provoked both fascination and scepticism. But when confronted with such complex and detailed theories, it is only natural that doubts arise.

For many, Basiago's claims are so full of specific and coherent detail that it is difficult to dismiss them out of hand. **The meticulous construction of his narrative** makes many think that, as incredible as it sounds, perhaps we should not reject it completely. After all, isn't it the job of the sceptic to question what seems all too obvious? And Basiago has a special ability to make even the most fanciful seem plausible, at least to his followers. But at the same time, **the lack of tangible evidence** and the inconsistencies in some aspects of his account have led others to believe that it might all be a fabrication too good to be true.

One of the most intriguing elements that fuels this speculation is the fact that Basiago claims that the **US government**, and more specifically **DARPA** (the Defence Advanced Research Projects Agency), not only developed this teleportation and time travel technology, but kept it **secret for decades**. This is where common conspiracy theories come into play: the idea that the government is hiding advanced technologies from the public is not new. In fact, **it's something that's been feeding conspiracy theory circles for years**.

Reality or well-constructed myth?

Basiago's story has inspired all sorts of speculation about how the government could have used this technology to **modify key historical events** or to monitor them, without intervening directly. If true, **Project Pegasus** would be part of a much larger effort to control the present and the future, as access to time-travel technology would radically change the rules of the game.

Some conspiracy theorists believe that the government has been using this technology to modify historical events, or at least observe them and extract vital information. If Project Pegasus is real, this would mean that the government could not only **predict** the future, but also change the past. This is more than enough to sustain the intrigue of those who firmly believe that **the government is hiding advanced technologies that would change life as we know it**.

Indeed, the idea that DARPA has had access to such technologies sounds like something out of a science fiction movie, but let's not forget that reality sometimes trumps fiction. **DARPA has been responsible for technological breakthroughs that seemed impossible** at the time, from early internet developments to innovations in robotics and military drones that, decades ago, seemed like something out of a futuristic dream. As such, many do not find it impossible that Project Pegasus was real and that the government somehow managed to keep it out of the public eye.

But why should we believe such an extraordinary story without hard evidence? **This is where the waters get muddied**. Basiago's critics point to the **lack of physical evidence** to back up his claims. Despite the wealth of detail he provides, he has been unable to offer documentary evidence or witnesses to confirm his involvement in Project Pegasus. And while his account has gained supporters, many of them have also been unable to provide information to back it up beyond Basiago's claims.

For many sceptics, claims of **time travel** and Mars missions are simply too fantastic to be credible. Critics insist that **the absence of official documents or physical evidence** suggests that it is all a figment of an active imagination or, perhaps, a desire for notoriety. After all, current science offers no solid support for the possibility of time travel, and while theories of quantum teleportation exist, we are still a long way from applying these ideas to human beings or interplanetary travel.

The history of top secret projects

Yet despite the lack of evidence, Basiago has found his **niche of loyal followers**, people who firmly believe that the US government has been involved in secret time manipulation projects for decades. This scepticism is not new. During the Cold War, for example, the US government carried out a **host of top-secret projects**, many of which are now public knowledge, such as **Project MKUltra**, a programme that involved mind-control experiments conducted on citizens without their consent. Such revelations, once dismissed as conspiracies, have helped to reinforce the belief that **other, more extraordinary projects may also be real**, just waiting to be declassified one day.

In that sense, Project Pegasus could be seen as the next revelation in a long line of secrets that the government would eventually admit to, as it did with MKUltra. For Basiago's supporters, this would be nothing new, but only **the confirmation of a larger truth**: that there are many technologies and projects that are kept hidden from the public for what the government claims are "national security" reasons.

A great imagined story?

However, it is also possible that Basiago is simply someone with an **overflowing imagination** who has managed to create a narrative so detailed that it is difficult to ignore. In this vein, **his narrative could be seen as a representation of our collective obsession with government secrets** and advanced technologies that have yet to be revealed to the public. Perhaps Project Pegasus is less a concrete reality and more a **metaphor for our desire to believe that the government has access to knowledge and tools that would completely change our understanding of the world**.

In a world where technology is advancing by leaps and bounds, it is easy to imagine that there is something beyond what we know. Basiago, with its story of time travel, missions to Mars and encounters with extraterrestrial beings, offers a narrative that satisfies that desire to **explore the unknown** and to believe that **science fiction is closer to reality than we think**.

After all, conspiracy stories not only fascinate us because of the possibility that they are true, but because they **feed our imagination**. They allow us to consider the possibility that there is **more than meets the eye**, that we live in a world where the rules might not be as rigid as they seem. So, while some dismiss Basiago as a mere narrator of fantasies, others see him as a figure who invites us to keep asking ourselves: **What if?**

3.3 Community impact and alternative theories

Andrew Basiago's account of Project Pegasus has had a significant impact on the community of paranormal enthusiasts and conspiracy theorists. On internet forums and at conferences, his story has been discussed, debated and, in many cases, defended by those who believe there may be some truth to his claims. While some see his story as pure fantasy, many others have proposed alternative theories to explain the more implausible elements of Basiago's account.

One of the main drivers of the impact of this narrative is **the viral effect it has had in the internet age**. Before the rise of the web, stories like Basiago's would have remained in small circles, limited by the capacity for dissemination. However, with the advent of forums, social media and video platforms, the story of Project Pegasus has spread rapidly. Today, thousands of people can learn its story in a matter of minutes, sharing and debating its details. As more people discover its story, the discussion grows, fuelled by the **ongoing interaction between sceptics, believers and the curious** that fuels the online narrative.

This has allowed Basiago's story to have a longer life than perhaps it would have had in an earlier era. Digital platforms have not only served as a channel for Basiago to expose his story, but have also allowed **new versions and reinterpretations** of his story to emerge. Each user can contribute something different, creating a space where Basiago's story is kept alive and constantly evolving.

From a psychological point of view, this can be understood as part of **human nature to seek answers** in times of uncertainty. Conspiracy theories, such as those surrounding Project Pegasus, provide a **sense of order and control** in a world that often seems chaotic. For many, these narratives offer an alternative explanation for events that otherwise seem inexplicable. Basiago is not only a character who tells a story; for some, he becomes a figure who offers **answers** to questions that official institutions fail to address.

It is precisely in these times of institutional distrust that theories like Basiago's thrive. In an era where government scandals and leaks like **Edward Snowden**'s and **Julian Assange'**s have revealed secrets that have been hidden for years, the possibility of secret projects like Project Pegasus seems more plausible to certain sectors of the population. This creates fertile ground for such stories to not only flourish, but to find an audience that welcomes them with open arms.

Another reason behind the lasting impact of Basiago's story is **the influence of science fiction** on popular culture. Teleportation, time travel and contact with extraterrestrial beings are recurring themes in books, films and series. Basiago's story borrows from these elements and presents them as fact, creating a curious mix of fiction and reality. In this sense, his story resonates with those who have already been influenced by decades of science fiction that, in many cases, anticipated technological advances that later became reality.

Where do we draw the line between science fiction and reality? Basiago's story raises precisely that question. We live in an age where technologies are advancing so fast that what was once considered fantasy is now possible. That is why, for many, Basiago's claims do not seem as far-fetched as they would have a few decades ago. In fact, science fiction has historically been **a source of inspiration for** real scientific developments. Advances that once seemed impossible are now part of our everyday lives, and that, in part, is what fuels belief in stories like Project Pegasus.

One of the most common theories that has been proposed to explain Basiago's account is that it may have been part of a **government psychological experiment**, designed to observe how subjects would react to extraordinary experiences and how malleable their perception of reality might be. Such experiments would not be new in the history of the US government. **Project MKUltra**, for example, involved a series of mind control experiments conducted on citizens without their consent. Basiago's memories, according to this theory, could have been induced by these methods of psychological manipulation, which would explain why he truly believes he was part of Project Pegasus, even if his experiences were the result of mental intervention rather than actual time travel.

There are also those who suggest that the cultural and social impact of the Basiago story is itself **a viral experiment**. In the same way that other mysteries in the digital age, such as the story of **John Titor** (an alleged time traveller who appeared on forums in the early 2000s), captured the public imagination, Basiago's story has spread not only because of its content, but because of the way people interact with it. Forums and blogs dedicated to paranormal phenomena continue to discuss his story, expanding on the details, reinterpreting them and generating new theories from them.

Moreover, **Basiago's cultural impact** goes beyond initial curiosity. His story has motivated others to investigate further into **top-secret government projects** and to formulate their own theories about **time control** and advanced technology that has not yet been revealed to the public. For many, Basiago's account is not only an entertaining story, but an **inspiration** to delve deeper into the hidden history of government experiments and to explore the limits of what is possible in the realm of technology and science.

Basiago's story also reflects the growing distrust of official institutions. Figures like him, although not whistleblowers in the traditional sense, have been perceived as those who reveal a **hidden truth** to the public. This is something we have seen with figures such as **Edward Snowden**, who revealed classified information, or **Julian Assange** with WikiLeaks. Although Basiago has no documentary evidence to back up his story, his narrative appeals to that same sense that there is something greater that the public does not know, a hidden truth waiting to be discovered.

Finally, one of the reasons why Basiago's story remains relevant is because it raises **philosophical questions** that go beyond its veracity. His story invites us to reflect on the **control of destiny**, the manipulation of time and the role of governments in advanced technology. Even if his story is not real, it leaves us with the intrigue of what would happen if it ever was. Conspiracy stories persist because they touch on deeply human themes: fear of the unknown, fascination with what might be beyond our understanding, and the idea that there are unseen forces controlling more than we know.

In short, Andrew Basiago and his account of Project Pegasus have left an indelible mark on **modern conspiracy culture**. Although the veracity of his claims remains highly contested, the impact of his story on the community remains strong, fuelling debates about teleportation, time travel and the possible use of advanced technologies that have yet to be revealed to the general public. Whether its story is seen as fact or well-crafted fiction, what is undeniable is that it has captured the **collective imagination** and inspired many to question the limits of what is possible.

Chapter 4: Mike "Madman" Marcum: The Inventor who Disappeared

The story of **Mike "Madman" Marcum** remains one of the most fascinating and mysterious in the field of **home experiments** and frontier science. In the 1990s, a period when technology was beginning to play a predominant role in everyday life, characters emerged from obscurity who captured public attention for their attempts to push the boundaries of science to previously unseen extremes. And among these characters, Marcum stands out as a legendary figure, someone who rose to fame for his bold claims and boundless ambition: the creation of a machine capable of opening a **portal through time**.

Born in Missouri, Marcum was not a trained scientist, but an ingenious, self-taught young man who, from an early age, showed an obsession with understanding the laws of physics and manipulating electromagnetic forces. Rather than follow the traditional paths of academia, he chose to explore his theories in his own home, experimenting with easily accessible but potentially dangerous technology. This approach earned him his nickname **"Madman"**, a reference to both his daring and the risky nature of his experiments.

In the mid-1990s, the fascination with the mysteries of physics and time travel was not just the stuff of science fiction novels or movies. **Radio shows like "Coast to Coast AM"**, where paranormal and conspiracy theories were regularly discussed, fed the curiosity of thousands of listeners looking for answers beyond the conventional. It was in this context that Marcum began to gain notoriety. With a charismatic personality and stories that defied the imagination, he soon became a recurring guest on radio programmes specialising in paranormal topics.

His story not only captured the imagination of those who dreamed of the possibility of **time travel**, but also sparked a debate about the **dangers of home experimentation** and the ethical limits of individual research. Unlike formal scientists, working under strict security frameworks and supervision, Marcum operated from the freedom (and risks) of his own backyard. His experiments, while full of ingenuity, were also extremely dangerous, which inevitably attracted the attention of the authorities.

The **electromagnetic fields** Marcum was playing with were not mere curiosities, but powerful forces that, if misused, could cause serious damage. But for Mike, the risk was worth it if it meant he could test his theory that it was possible to open a portal in space-time. His reasoning was simple but intriguing: if enough energy could be generated, it might be able to distort the very fabric of time itself. This concept, though taken directly from science fiction, had some basis in Einstein's theory of relativity, which suggests that space and time are interconnected and can be manipulated under the right conditions.

However, what really pushed Marcum to the limit was not only his ambition, but his **lack of resources**. Despite his determination and willingness to take risks, the technology he possessed was not enough to achieve the level of energy needed for his project. This desire for more energy led him to make decisions that would get him in trouble with the law. The theft of high-powered transformers to power his machine was a critical point in his history, marking the moment when his ambition became a threat not only to himself, but also to his environment.

His eventual **arrest**, far from dampening public curiosity, only further stoked interest in his story. Was Mike Marcum a **misunderstood genius**, someone whose intellect and vision were simply ahead of their time? Or was he a **reckless young man**, playing with forces beyond his comprehension, putting his life and the lives of others at risk? Opinions were divided. For some, Marcum represented the dream of all those who once dreamed of bending the rules of the universe. To others, he was a **warning** of the dangers of unchecked amateur science.

Over time, theories and speculation about his fate grew. While some people mocked his failed attempts, others saw him as a **tragic hero**, someone who might have been on the verge of achieving the impossible before his mysterious disappearance. Was he a victim of his own invention, trapped somewhere in time or space? Or did he simply disappear for more earthly reasons, perhaps seeking to avoid further legal trouble or escape public pressure?

Mike "Madman" Marcum left an ambiguous but captivating legacy. His story continues to inspire amateur scientists and conspiracists alike, while his ultimate fate remains a mystery. Marcum represents the kind of character who, through his audacity and obsession, manages to transform a personal curiosity into a **modern legend**. But in the end, his disappearance raises a question that remains unanswered: **How far did he really go?**

4.1 Experiments that led to his arrest

It all began in the early 1990s, when **Mike Marcum**, at the age of 21, embarked on a scientific adventure that would lead to fame and, ultimately, arrest. Rather than conforming to the conventional laws of physics, Marcum sought to **manipulate time** with a homemade device inspired by what he called a **"vortex generator"**. His idea, while ambitious, was simple: use extremely powerful **electromagnetic fields** to create a temporal portal that would allow him to travel through time. What began as a homemade experiment with basic tools soon became a story that would capture the imagination of many.

The first experiments in your backyard

Marcum set up his **experimental platform** in the backyard of his Missouri home, using components he had assembled or improvised. His theory was based on misunderstood ideas from **quantum physics** and space-time manipulation. He believed that if he could generate a strong enough electromagnetic field, he could **open a wormhole** or distort the fabric of space-time enough to send objects through it.

Initially, Marcum started with small, easy-to-handle objects. He would throw screws, coins and other small materials into the area where his generator was operating. According to his account, the objects disappeared completely after being subjected to the effects of the electromagnetic field, which, to him, meant that **something was happening**, although he did not know exactly what. This supposed disappearance of the small objects was interpreted by Marcum as a sign that he was on the right track towards creating a time portal.

Such home experiments were dangerous not only because he was manipulating **electromagnetic fields** without proper supervision or safety equipment, but also because Marcum himself did not have a full technical understanding of the phenomena he was dealing with. Despite this, his enthusiasm and conviction drove him on. For him, the risks were secondary to the possibility of making a **revolutionary discovery**.

The energy dilemma: the tipping point

As his experiments progressed, Marcum realised that the power of his equipment was not enough to achieve the kind of **temporal effect** he was looking for. Although he had achieved some results with small objects, he knew he would need **much more power** to make the machine work on a large scale, perhaps enough to send a human being through the portal.

This is where the dilemma that would change the course of his story arose. With limited resources and no access to advanced technology, Marcum faced an insurmountable obstacle: **he needed more power**. Domestic technology could not generate the amount of electricity his machine required to amplify the electromagnetic field. Without the means to purchase industrial transformers, he made a drastic decision.

Marcum decided to steal transformers from a nearby power plant. These transformers, designed to handle high-voltage electrical currents, could supply the amount of power he believed his generator needed. With these devices, he hoped to amplify his machine and create a vortex large enough to span space-time. However, the theft did not go unnoticed by the authorities. The stolen transformers were quickly traced back to him, and Marcum was **arrested for theft**.

This was a key moment in his life, not only because he was facing criminal charges, but because the arrest **catapulted his story to fame**. What could have been just an eccentric backyard experiment became a national story of interest. Marcum went from a young man with big dreams and limited resources to a public figure, known for his bold attempt to defy the laws of physics.

The impact of his arrest and his appearance in the media

Although his time in prison was brief, the arrest did not dampen his ambition. During his imprisonment, Marcum continued to defend his experiments and theories. Despite his run-in with the law, he never gave up the idea that he was **close to achieving time travel**. His unflinching attitude in the face of adversity, coupled with the **mystery** surrounding his experiments, generated a growing interest in his story.

At this time, the impact of the media began to play a crucial role in building the Marcum myth. One of the factors that most contributed to his fame was his participation in the **radio programme "Coast to Coast AM"**. This show, hosted by the charismatic host **Art Bell**, was known for its discussions of paranormal phenomena, conspiracy theories and unexplained events. For fans of such programmes, Marcum was not just a young man with wild ideas; he was someone who, it seemed, had risked everything in his quest to understand the **mysteries of time**.

During his appearance on "Coast to Coast AM", Marcum explained in detail how he had come to the conclusion that electromagnetic fields could manipulate time. He recounted his early experiments and enthusiastically described his discoveries. This platform gave him access to a **mass audience**, and soon his story was known throughout the country. The mix of science fiction, technology and quasi-science fringe elements made Marcum **a cult figure** among paranormal buffs and conspiracy theorists.

From that point on, he began to receive **letters of support**, offers of collaboration and even funding proposals from people who wanted to see how far he could take his experiment. However, he also attracted **a multitude of sceptics** who pointed to the lack of tangible evidence to back up his claims. While some saw him as a **misunderstood genius**, others saw him as simply a reckless young man who had crossed a dangerous line.

The technical side: what did Marcum hope to achieve?

One of the most intriguing aspects of Marcum's story is the **technical nature of his "vortex generator"**. Although his ideas were unorthodox and lacked solid scientific backing, his device was designed to generate extremely powerful electromagnetic fields. Marcum's **goal** was to distort space-time enough to create a **wormhole** that could be used as a time portal.

Although these ideas seem straight out of science fiction, they had a **distant echo** in more formal physical theories. In **Einstein'**s theory of **relativity**, it is postulated that space and time are connected, and that under extreme conditions of gravity or energy, space-time can warp. Marcum believed he could replicate these effects on a smaller scale using his generator. However, **mainstream scientists** sharply criticised his experiments, pointing out that the conditions needed to create a wormhole were far more extreme than he could achieve with his homemade technology.

What is clear is that Marcum was experimenting with something dangerous. Strong **electromagnetic fields** can have unpredictable effects, and without proper safety precautions, Marcum's experiments could have caused significant harm, both to himself and to those around him. Fortunately, his arrest prevented him from conducting larger experiments that could have ended in tragedy.

Reaction from the scientific community and scepticism

While Marcum was enthusiastically received in some circles, the **scientific community** largely ignored him. Although some experts in electromagnetism commented on his ideas, pointing out that electromagnetic fields could cause strange phenomena under certain conditions, most dismissed his theories as **pseudoscience**. There was no concrete evidence to suggest that Marcum's experiments could actually manipulate time, and without the validation of peer-reviewed studies or verifiable evidence, his claims were seen as mere speculation.

However, this lack of scientific backing did not prevent his story from continuing to circulate. In fact, the disinterest of the official scientific community only served to reinforce the **belief in certain quarters** that Marcum was onto something important, something that the institutions wanted to keep hidden. For these believers, Marcum was no mere amateur; he was someone who had touched the boundaries of **forbidden science**.

4.2 His mysterious disappearance: A time traveller lost in time?

The real enigma surrounding **Mike "Madman" Marcum** lies not just in his eccentric experiments with electromagnetic fields and his attempts to create a time machine, but in what happened after he achieved some notoriety. In the late 1990s, in **1997**, Marcum disappeared from public view without a trace, and it is this mystery that has helped cement his status as an almost legendary figure.

According to sources close to Marcum, he was working on a **more advanced version** of his vortex generator. After his arrest and subsequent release, he had acquired better equipment, with more power and expanded capabilities. Many believe that Marcum was determined to take his experiment a step further, convinced that he might have been on the verge of achieving a **leap in time**. However, in an unexpected twist, one day he simply stopped appearing in public. There were no more interviews on radio shows, no new statements about his progress. Marcum, who had been relatively visible in the media, disappeared as if he had vanished into thin air.

Theories about his disappearance: accident or success?

With Marcum's disappearance, speculation soon followed. Some of the most common theories suggest that his absence could have been the result of a **tragic accident** due to the instability of the high-energy experiments he was conducting. It is well known that the electromagnetic fields Marcum was working with could be extremely dangerous, especially without proper safety protocols. In this scenario, it is possible that a fatal accident could have occurred, which would explain why he was never heard from again. However, in the absence of concrete evidence of an accident or the recovery of his body, this theory remains unconfirmed.

On the other hand, there are those who argue that Marcum may have **achieved his goal**: time travel. According to this version, his disappearance was not the result of an accident, but a direct consequence of having managed to open a time portal with his machine. Supporters of this theory believe that Marcum may have travelled to another time or even another dimension, but **lost the ability to return** to his original time. This narrative is more aligned with conspiracy theories, where Marcum becomes a tragic figure, a pioneer of time travel who ended up trapped at some unknown point in history.

A 1930s man with a strange device

Among the most popular stories circulating **on internet forums** that fuel the myth of Marcum's disappearance, there is one in particular that has gained a lot of attention. According to this theory, a man was found dead in the **1930s**, carrying a technological device that did not belong to that era. Rumours suggest that this unidentified man could have been Mike Marcum, who after a **failed experiment** would have travelled back in time, trapped there and with no means of returning to his own time.

While this story is fascinating, **there is no evidence** to support the idea that the man found in the 1930s was Marcum. Rather, it is a tale fuelled by imagination and the desire to find answers to a mystery that, to this day, remains unsolved. However, as with many mysteries in the paranormal realm, the lack of concrete evidence has not stopped believers from believing that Marcum may have been the victim of a temporary accident that threw him into another time.

The impact of disappearance on his legend

Marcum's disappearance has been the **key point** in the construction of his myth. Although there is no solid evidence that he actually travelled through time, the **lack of answers** about his whereabouts has continued to fuel speculation. It is his absence that has allowed his story to survive and spread over the years. Had he continued to be visible in the public sphere, his story might have fallen into oblivion, like so many other tales of amateur experimenters. But his disappearance left a **big question**

unanswered, and that void was quickly filled with theories and narratives that presented him as one of the few humans to have managed to manipulate time, albeit at the cost of his own fate.

What is interesting about Marcum's disappearance is how it has been **interpreted from different perspectives**. For some, his absence is a sign that he finally achieved the impossible. In this sense, he is compared to science fiction figures who cross the threshold of the known, paying the price for discovering a forbidden truth. For others, on the other hand, it is possible that Marcum simply decided to **disappear on his own**, either to avoid further legal problems or because of the growing pressures and expectations that had arisen around his figure.

A new "John Titor"?

Marcum's disappearance has also been compared to the **famous case of John Titor**, an alleged time traveller who appeared on internet forums in the early 2000s. Although there are no direct links between Marcum and Titor, some believe that Marcum may have been a precursor of sorts to Titor, or even the same person under a pseudonym. Both cases share common elements: a mysterious character who claims to have had access to advanced temporal technologies and an **unexplained disappearance** that has left fans wondering whether they really did time travel or simply fled from public life.

The comparison between Marcum and Titor has further fuelled the **mythology** surrounding both characters. While John Titor was almost certainly a fictional construct, the fact that Marcum was a real person lends a more tangible air to the possibility that something out of the ordinary may have actually happened with his disappearance.

The theory of voluntary withdrawal

Despite the more exciting theories suggesting time travel or fatal accidents, there is also a **more mundane interpretation** of Marcum's disappearance. Some speculate that, after media pressure and legal complications, Marcum simply decided to **retire from public life**. Perhaps he was overwhelmed by the expectations of those who believed he was on the verge of a monumental breakthrough, or perhaps financial or health problems forced him to step back. In this version, Marcum could be living a quiet, anonymous life, avoiding any attention related to his controversial fame.

However, if this is the case, his decision to completely disappear from any radar is equally intriguing. In today's age of social media, it is difficult for anyone to stay hidden, and if Marcum really did decide to withdraw from public life, his ability to do so so successfully has only further fuelled theories that something extraordinary happened to him.

The context of the 1990s: the rise of the conspiracies

It is impossible to understand Marcum's disappearance without considering the context in which he lived. The **1990s** was an era marked by the rise of **conspiracy theories**, fuelled in large part by the **growth of the internet** and **distrust of** government **institutions**. This era was key to the proliferation of stories like Marcum's, which spread rapidly among communities of amateur scientists, conspiracy theorists and paranormal enthusiasts.

In the 1990s, **conspiracies about secret technologies**, government projects and the manipulation of time captured the popular imagination. The lack of transparency in some sectors of the US government, along with events such as the revelations of **Project MKUltra** and other secret programmes, fostered the belief that there was **hidden knowledge** that the authorities did not want made public. Marcum's story fit perfectly into this environment. For many, his disappearance was interpreted as a sign that he had discovered something important and that "someone" wanted to silence him.

Reaction from the amateur science community

Marcum's disappearance had a significant impact on the **community of amateur scientists** and those experimenting with unconventional theories. For some, his disappearance was seen as a warning about the **dangers of crossing certain boundaries**. Marcum had not only captured the attention of the media, but had also begun to attract the attention of the authorities. This fact, combined with his disappearance, created an air of **caution** among those who were also interested in experiments with unconventional technologies.

On the other hand, many in this community saw Marcum as an **inspirational figure**, someone willing to risk everything to explore the mysteries of the universe. His story served as a warning, but also as an example of what can be achieved when one dares to go beyond the limits of what is considered scientifically acceptable. While some experimenters became more cautious after Marcum's demise, others felt compelled to continue their own work, motivated by the idea that there was still uncharted territory in the world of fringe science.

Possible government cover-up

Another popular theory that has circulated around Marcum's disappearance is the idea of a **government cover-up**. In this version, it is suggested that the US government or some other powerful entity may have intervened to stop Marcum's experiments. Proponents of this theory believe that Marcum may have discovered something **too dangerous** or potentially disruptive to be shared with the public, and that his disappearance was orchestrated to hide the knowledge he was developing.

Although this theory lacks concrete evidence, it is very much in line with popular **conspiracy narratives** of the time, in which the government is believed to have access to advanced technologies that have not been revealed to the general public. Some have even suggested that Marcum may have been forced to continue his work in secret, under the supervision of some **classified government agency**, which would explain his complete disappearance from the public sphere.

Marcum's legacy in unconventional science

Despite the doubts surrounding the veracity of his experiments and the nature of his demise, Mike Marcum's story has left a lasting mark on the field of **unconventional science**. Although his methods were rudimentary and lacked the usual scientific rigour, his **imagination and determination** have inspired a new generation of scientists and amateurs. For many, Marcum's real legacy is not whether or not he succeeded in time travel, but the fact that he dared to challenge the **limits of human knowledge**.

Today, his story is still told on internet forums and paranormal radio programmes, and his name is mentioned alongside other pioneers who have explored the **frontiers of science**, albeit from the fringes. Despite his passing, Marcum remains a **source of inspiration** for those who believe that the universe still holds secrets that can be uncovered with the right tools and an open mind.

4.3 The science behind his experiments: Is it replicable?

The most intriguing component of **Mike Marcum'**s story is whether the experiments he conducted have any real scientific basis. While the narrative surrounding his efforts has been popularised in alternative media and conspiracy circles, the question remains: **did his experiments have any scientific validity?** The details of exactly how his machine worked are not entirely clear, but the descriptions he offered suggest that he was **experimenting with intense electromagnetic fields** and technology related to the use of **high-voltage transformers**.

What Marcum seemed to be looking for was the possibility of generating an **electromagnetic vortex** that could somehow create a shortcut in **space-time**, allowing him to travel through time or even teleport. However, from a scientific perspective, this requires analysing the fundamentals behind such ideas, mainly within the framework of theoretical physics and technological limitations.

The foundations of relativity theory and wormholes

One of the central aspects of speculation about time travel and the warping of space-time comes from Einstein's **theory of general relativity**. This theory states that space and time are interconnected, forming what we call **spacetime**, and that spacetime can be **curved** or **distorted** under the influence of gravity or large amounts of energy. In fact, relativity posits that, theoretically, under extremely specific conditions, it would be possible to create what is known as a **wormhole**, a shortcut through space-time that could connect two distant points in the universe, or even two moments in time.

Science fiction has adopted these concepts as one of the bases for many time travel stories, but the reality is that **creating a** viable **wormhole** would require amounts of energy that are almost **unimaginable** with today's technology. We are talking about energy levels equivalent to that emitted by a **black hole** or a **supernova**, something that certainly cannot be achieved in a domestic backyard environment. The very concept of travelling through a wormhole, while mathematically plausible, has not yet been experimentally demonstrated, and **wormholes** remain a **theoretical speculation** within physics.

What Marcum was doing, while ingenious from an amateur's perspective, was much closer to amateur experimental science than to **today's scientific concepts** related to wormhole creation or time manipulation. According to his own descriptions, his machine used **electromagnetic fields** generated by industrial transformers to create a temporal effect. Although **electromagnetic fields** can have remarkable effects on particles at the subatomic level, as we have seen in experiments with particle accelerators, the kind of space-time manipulation Marcum was aiming for is a far cry from what is possible with home-made transformers and generators.

Electromagnetism and its effects on matter

To understand Marcum's experiments, it is important to note that **electromagnetism** plays a central role in many phenomena in modern physics. We know that **electromagnetic fields** can influence charged particles and that they are central to many of today's technological processes, such as electricity transmission, telecommunications and particle accelerators. However, the **electromagnetic interactions** that Marcum was trying to harness would theoretically require a much more advanced level of control and energy than he could achieve with his equipment.

One hypothesis that has been put forward is that Marcum may have generated some unusual electromagnetic phenomena, such as **electrical discharges** or **plasma effects**. These phenomena, while impressive, are not related to **time distortion**. In addition, **strong electromagnetic fields** can cause adverse effects on the environment, such as interference in electronic devices, and can even, under certain conditions, affect human perception, causing **hallucinations** or **strange sensations**. This could explain some of the experiences Marcum described, but does not necessarily indicate that he was manipulating space-time.

The question of the energy required

One of the biggest problems in replicating Marcum's experiments is the **amount of energy** that would be needed to achieve a significant manipulation of space-time. As mentioned above, to create an effect that distorts time or space would require **energy levels** that we can only observe in extreme astrophysical phenomena. The generators and transformers that Marcum used, while powerful at the household level, do not have the capacity to even approach these magnitudes.

Physicists who have commented on their work point out that, while **electromagnetic fields** can have some curious effects under certain conditions, creating a time vortex or portal would require the kind of energy that we could only generate with advanced nuclear fusion reactors or technologies that have not yet been developed.

Could your work be replicated?

The science behind Marcum's experiments continues to fascinate **science enthusiasts** and **conspiracy theorists** alike. Although it has so far not been proven that his machine had the ability to manipulate time, there is still interest in **extreme electromagnetic phenomena** and how they might influence our understanding of space and time. While it is true that wormholes and time travel have not been replicated or demonstrated, this does not mean that physics does not continue to explore the **frontiers of knowledge**.

Some physicists are studying how **extreme magnetic fields** might affect the behaviour of subatomic particles and whether, under certain controlled conditions, anomalies in space-time could be created. While this research is still in the very early stages, it shows that science is still searching for answers to fundamental questions about the **universe** and the **nature of time**.

Indeed, it has been speculated that if in the future we succeed in developing much more advanced energy sources - such as **nuclear fusion** reactors or complete control of **antimatter -** we could come close to some of the theoretical concepts that today seem possible only in the realm of science fiction.

Marcum's legacy in unconventional science

Despite the lack of clear evidence that his experiments had any solid scientific foundation, Mike Marcum's story has inspired a new generation of **dreamers** and **unconventional scientists** to continue exploring the limits of the possible. While the **mainstream scientific community** has been largely sceptical, **amateur scientists** and **conspiracy theorists** continue to speculate about how advances in the control of energy and electromagnetism could one day lead to a new era of discovery, including the manipulation of time.

The fascination with Marcum's work lies in his willingness to **risk everything** to explore an unknown frontier, even with limited means and incomplete knowledge. In many ways, Marcum represents the figure of the **amateur scientist** who dares to challenge the norms, inspired by science fiction and fringe theories. Although current science does not support his claims, his story remains a source of **inspiration** for those seeking to understand the deeper mysteries of the universe.

Chapter 5: Andrew Carlssin: The Millionaire Investor of the Future

The story of Andrew Carlssin is one of the most mysterious and fascinating legends to have circulated in the world of **financial conspiracies** and **time travellers**. At the heart of this story lies a claim so extraordinary that it defies any notion of what we consider possible: a seemingly ordinary man who, overnight, turns **$800 into $350 million**, getting his stock market investments right time and time again. How could someone with so few resources achieve such a feat in such a short time, in such a volatile market?

What makes this story even more fascinating is the **explanation** Carlssin himself offered when he was arrested: he claimed that he was not an ordinary man, but a **time traveller** from the year 2256. According to him, he used his **advanced knowledge** of stock market events to profit from fluctuations that were well known to him, since by his time they were history. Carlssin claimed that he simply took advantage of investment opportunities in such a way that it was impossible to fail, as he knew the future results. This claim, while unbelievable to many, raises troubling questions about the **boundary between science and fiction**, and whether it is really possible for someone to have mastered **time travel** for personal gain.

However, as is often the case in the best conspiracy stories, things quickly became complicated. Despite the fantastic nature of his confession, Carlssin mysteriously disappeared, leaving behind more questions than answers. Not only did his sudden disappearance fuel speculation about his origin, but also the lack of concrete information about his existence before the incident and his whereabouts after the events. There are no clear records of his life before he appeared on the stock exchange, which has led many to wonder whether he was really flesh and blood or part of an **elaborate conspiracy** designed to conceal something much bigger.

This introduction focuses not only on Carlssin as an enigmatic figure, but also on the broader framework in which this story unfolded. The stock market, with its unpredictability and complexities, has long been the subject of speculation about its manipulation by conventional and unusual methods. The idea of a **time traveller** exploiting the financial system with inside information from another century captures the imagination and reflects our own **fears and desires**: the possibility of controlling the future or discovering that someone else has already done so.

This chapter explores not only the incredible story of Andrew Carlssin, but also the **interventions** of the US Securities and Exchange Commission (SEC) that attempted to unravel this mysterious case, and finally, the **debate as** to whether it was all a **cleverly crafted fraud**, an **urban myth** that got out of control, or whether we really are dealing with the first **documented time traveller**.

5.1 The story of the man who predicted the market

The origin of the **Andrew Carlssin** legend begins in January 2003, when the US **Securities and Exchange Commission (SEC)** arrested a man who had achieved the unthinkable: making **126 stock market investments in a row** without failing once. This fact alone defies logic, as even the most experienced investors cannot accurately predict how the market will behave on so many occasions. Carlssin had started with a **modest investment of $800**, but within a couple of weeks, that sum had grown to a staggering **$350 million**. His flawless and uninterrupted successes immediately caught the attention of the SEC, which soon launched a thorough investigation into his trading.

From the perspective of the SEC agents, Carlssin's behaviour could not have been more suspicious. The **odds** of anyone pulling off such a perfect series of investments, without any losses, were virtually **impossible**. Indeed, some analysts went so far as to estimate that the chance of this happening without inside information was **one in a quadrillion**. The level of accuracy he demonstrated in his investments only seemed possible if Carlssin had access to confidential information or was involved in a **massive financial fraud**. So SEC agents acted quickly, believing they had stumbled upon one of the most elaborate market manipulation schemes ever seen.

What investigators did not expect, however, was the **incredible defence** Carlssin offered once he was questioned. Instead of denying the allegations or admitting to being involved in fraud, Carlssin surprised everyone with an even more disconcerting statement: he claimed to be a **time traveller** from the **year 2256**. According to his account, his success in the stock market was not due to any illicit scheme, but to his **advanced knowledge** of future stock market events. To him, the fluctuations that were unpredictable to contemporary investors were as clear as a history book.

This kind of confession was obviously greeted with **incredulity**. The story of a man travelling back in time to profit from the stock market seemed more like something out of a science fiction novel than an interrogation room. However, Carlssin not only stuck to his story, but also **detailed** with surprising accuracy several future market events that had not yet unfolded at the time, further baffling investigators. According to some reports, Carlssin was able to predict stock market movements that were later confirmed, leading some to question whether his story, however improbable, could have any truth to it.

To further complicate the case, Carlssin also offered **extraordinary information** on subjects completely unrelated to the stock market. He is said to have attempted to negotiate his release by providing crucial details about **Osama bin Laden'**s location and suggesting that he knew the **cure for AIDS**. Although these claims are difficult to verify, the fact that Carlssin had attempted to offer this information to save himself from financial charges perplexed investigators. The scale of the promises he was making was so improbable that the authorities did not know how to react.

The context behind the investments and the mystery of the market

To understand the **magnitude** of Carlssin's achievement from a technical point of view, it is important to consider how the **stock market** works. In an environment as volatile as the stock market, where investment decisions are affected by a myriad of unpredictable factors - from political decisions to global economic shifts - even the most skilled investors often make mistakes. **Market ups and downs** are the result of a complex web of interactions between supply, demand, investor psychology and external events.

Continuous stock market successes, such as those achieved by Carlssin, not only imply absolute mastery of **financial dynamics**, but also defy the laws of **chance**. Even the most advanced algorithms of the time, used by large corporations to predict market behaviour, would not have been able to maintain a perfect record like his. This brings us to the central question: if Carlssin had no **inside information**, how was he able to predict market movements so perfectly?

For some, the most logical explanation is that **he manipulated** market information in some way. But the curious thing is that the SEC could find no evidence of **collusion** between Carlssin and any entity that provided him with inside information. His personal history showed no sign of prior wealth or connection to the financial world, further complicating the investigation.

The authorities' disbelief and attempts at negotiation

Despite Carlssin's implausible claims, SEC investigators remained **sceptical**. It was easier to assume that this was a fraud scheme than to accept the idea that Carlssin could be a time traveller with privileged knowledge. However, the lack of clear background on his earlier life and his subsequent disappearance cast a shadow of doubt.

Some reports later suggested that Carlssin had tried to offer the authorities a **series of deals in** exchange for his release. Among his promises was the revelation of **future technologies** that he claimed would revolutionise the world. He also offered to detail medical and scientific breakthroughs that would occur in the next century, all in the hope that researchers would see him as more than just a con man. But these claims were met with incredulity, and there is no record of these offers ever being accepted or verified.

What puzzled the researchers most, however, was the **lack of prior information** about Carlssin. There were no solid records of his life prior to the stock market events, and no documents indicating his presence in the financial world prior to his first investment. His **personal history** was a mystery, which added an additional layer of intrigue to his case. Could someone have created a fictitious identity to execute such a perfect scheme, or did Carlssin really come from a future time where all these events had already happened?

5.2 The intervention of the SEC and its mysterious disappearance

Andrew Carlssin's arrest provoked a mixture of disbelief and fascination in the media. Initial reports were merely fragments of information that fuelled rumours: a man had been arrested by the US Securities and Exchange Commission (SEC) after making a series of extraordinarily successful investments. In a short time, Carlssin had managed to turn a modest sum of money into hundreds of millions, all the while claiming that his knowledge came from the future.

At first, the authorities treated him like any other financial fraud suspect, albeit with an added dose of scepticism. His excuse - dating back to 2256 - seemed more like a poor defence or a desperate attempt to divert attention. However, as the investigation progressed, more disturbing details began to emerge, causing some agents to question whether there was really more to his words.

The SEC, instead of dismissing the case outright, decided to subject Carlssin to a series of interrogations. This is where the story becomes more intriguing. According to sources close to the case, during these interrogations, Carlssin was able to accurately predict the outcome of future stock market fluctuations and major economic events, despite being completely incommunicado and without access to information from the outside world. This detail, which was never officially acknowledged by the authorities, has been the subject of debate in certain conspiracy theorist circles.

However, the most inexplicable was yet to come. After his arrest, Carlssin was released on bail... and then disappeared without a trace. No record of his whereabouts, no contact with his lawyers and no trace of his activities in the financial system. He simply vanished. The SEC, which had initially promised to investigate the case thoroughly, kept a mysterious silence that only fuelled speculation.

Stock market impact

The impact of Carlssin's financial activities did not go unnoticed in the stock market world. His uncanny ability to foresee market movements generated a wave of suspicion among investors and regulators. Reports indicated that he had made extremely risky bets on companies that other experts considered to be on the verge of collapse, but which, against all odds, rebounded significantly just after Carlssin invested in them.

Investment experts began to analyse his trades, looking for some secret strategy or pattern that they could replicate, but all that was discovered was an apparent lack of logic in his choices. However, all that was discovered was the apparent lack of logic in his choices, which generated further astonishment. How could someone, without access to inside information, make such accurate predictions? Some theorists began to suggest that Carlssin's disappearance might be connected to larger forces within the financial system that did not want his methods to be made public.

The psychological effect on the market was remarkable. In the days following his disappearance, there was a brief but tangible sense of uncertainty. The financial media constantly discussed the case, and many investors began to act more cautiously, wondering whether there were more people like Carlssin trading with "impossible" knowledge. This brief period of paranoia caused a slight slowdown in risky investments, with some investors opting for more conservative strategies until the dust settled.

However, the effects were not long-term. The authorities tried to minimise the impact of his accurate predictions, calling his actions a "lucky fraud" and declaring that he was simply a con artist who had played on market volatility. Despite these efforts to quell concerns, the enigma surrounding Carlssin planted a small seed of doubt as to whether, somewhere, advanced information beyond current market knowledge might exist.

Rumours of market manipulation by Carlssin

As more theories emerged, some investors and financial theorists began to suspect that Carlssin had not only predicted the market, but perhaps actively manipulated it. His ability to anticipate specific events and make key investments at critical moments led some to believe that his actions somehow caused ripple effects that altered the natural course of markets.

Speculation began to emerge that Carlssin may have executed trades large enough to trigger fluctuations in particular stocks, leading other investors to unwittingly follow the pattern and increase volatility. Although this theory was never proven, the fact that some market movements coincided with his investments generated further speculation about the extent of his knowledge or, perhaps, his ability to somehow control the behaviour of financial markets.

SEC silence as a sign of a cover-up

The SEC's silence on the case was, to many, as disconcerting as Carlssin's disappearance. The Securities and Exchange Commission, known for being transparent and extremely rigorous in its handling of financial fraud cases, adopted a strangely secretive stance. Such behaviour was highly unusual, especially in a high-profile case that had captured the media's attention.

Analysts began to compare the Carlssin case to other large-scale financial frauds, where the SEC had acted swiftly and clearly, issuing detailed reports and conducting thorough investigations. In the Carlssin case, however, public information was scarce and the investigation seemed to have faded after his disappearance. This information vacuum was interpreted by some as a clear sign that something else was at play, perhaps a cover-up related to information that should not be made public.

Some SEC critics went so far as to suggest that the Commission had been pressured by outside forces, possibly government agencies, to prevent further details of the case from being released. The fact that key documents related to the investigation were never released further fuelled theories of a cover-up.

Reactions in international markets

Carlssin's demise not only generated a wave of uncertainty on Wall Street, but also had an impact on international markets. Investors in Europe, Asia and Latin America began to speculate about the implications of Carlssin's financial predictions and movements. In particular, several international investment funds began to investigate whether there was any relationship between movements in US markets and their own.

In emerging markets, where volatility is already part of the normal landscape, Carlssin's story set off alarm bells. Several international banks became interested in investigating his movements on Wall Street, trying to decipher whether his transactions might have influenced the stability of smaller markets. Although no conclusive evidence was found that Carlssin had directly affected international markets, the fact that his name was mentioned in these circles showed the global reach of his demise.

Academic interest in the case

The mystery surrounding Andrew Carlssin also captured the interest of certain academic circles. Economists, financial market experts and academics interested in behavioural economics began to analyse his case from different angles. Some suggested that Carlssin might have used an extremely advanced methodology to predict market movements that others could not see. This led to several conferences and studies trying to understand whether his success was the result of some hidden theory of market behaviour or simply an anomaly.

Behavioural economists tried to apply theoretical models to Carlssin's investment patterns, looking for any hint of logic that might explain his apparent "superhuman" knowledge. While many concluded that it was impossible to obtain his level of precision without access to inside information, others continued to explore the possibility that there was an underlying strategy not yet understood by traditional financial systems. Carlssin's case became a recurring theme at economics and finance conferences, where the enigma of his investments continues to be the subject of academic debate.

5.3 Fraud, myth or real traveller?

From the moment Andrew Carlssin disappeared, the big question that has remained up in the air is whether he was really a financial fraud genius, a master con artist, or, as he claimed in his bizarre confession, a true time traveller. His story has inspired all sorts of theories, ranging from the rational to the fantastic. But the lack of concrete evidence in either direction has kept this legend alive in the minds of those drawn to the unexplained.

Financial fraud theory: A fraudster with a brilliant plan?

For the more sceptical, the most logical explanation is that Carlssin was simply a con man with an extremely well-planned strategy. His ability to turn a small sum of money into hundreds of millions could be explained as the result of a series of high-risk bets that, by pure chance, worked out well. This theory holds that Carlssin would have taken advantage of market volatility at a crucial moment, choosing companies whose movements were difficult to predict, making his successes seem miraculous.

Some financial experts have suggested that Carlssin may have had access to inside information, which would explain his extremely accurate investments. Although illegal, insider trading is a known practice and, in some cases, difficult to detect. However, this theory does not explain how he could have achieved so much success in so many different investments without raising suspicions beforehand.

Some speculate that the level of precision in his investments may have been the result of hidden connections to financial market insider networks, allowing him to trade in areas where confidential information gave him an unfair advantage. But such trades usually attract attention, and the fact that Carlssin remained so discreet until he had amassed millions suggests that, if there was a fraud, it was executed with a level of sophistication that few others have achieved.

Advanced Algorithm Theory: Software that no one else has?

Another theory that has gained popularity among more technical financial circles is the idea that Carlssin was not a time traveller, but someone with access to technology that, at the time, was unknown to the general public. Some suggest that he may have developed or gained access to extremely advanced predictive software or algorithms that allowed him to anticipate market movements with astonishing accuracy.

In the world of finance, trading algorithms have transformed the way markets are traded, but at the time Carlssin made his appearance, these tools were not as well developed. However, some believe that he may have had access to a prototype version of some predictive software that no one else knew about.

The idea behind this theory is that somehow Carlssin had the ability to detect hidden patterns in market data that others simply could not see. This would have been possible if he had a system capable of processing vast amounts of information and extrapolating future trends with a high degree of certainty. While it sounds incredible, Carlssin's story aligns with the current aspirations of the financial world, where investors are continually looking for ways to predict market behaviour through the use of artificial intelligence and big data.

So far, no such technology has come to light, and some believe that, if Carlssin had access to it, he may have hidden it after his disappearance. This speculation continues to fuel the narrative that the real mystery is not so much whether Carlssin was a time traveller, but whether he had in his hands a predictive tool that could change the future of finance forever.

The Urban Myth: A Contemporary Legend?

For those who prefer a simpler explanation, Carlssin was nothing more than a fictitious character, the product of urban legends circulating on the internet and in the tabloid media. In fact, the lack of hard evidence and the absence of official records of his existence fuel the possibility that this story was fabricated from the beginning.

The story first appeared in a publication of dubious credibility, the WEEKLY WORLD NEWS, a tabloid known for publishing outlandish stories that are later revealed to be false. This source, along with the extraordinary nature of the story, has led many to assume that the whole case is at best an exaggeration, and at worst a complete fabrication.

However, the fact that the SEC has never issued a definitive statement denying the case has left room for speculation to continue. Was it simply a myth that got out of hand, or was there something else that led the authorities to remain silent?

The fascinating thing about urban legends is that even when the evidence seems to disprove the story, the mystery remains. Gaps in official information, the SEC's silence, and Carlssin's disappearance have helped this story transcend its origin as a simple tabloid article and become one of the most persistent legends of the 21st century.

The real time traveller?

And, of course, we cannot ignore the most fantastic theory: that Carlssin really was a time traveller. Those who believe in this possibility argue that his incredible market knowledge cannot be explained with today's analytical tools. Carlssin's ability to anticipate financial movements so accurately is seen by some as proof that he had access to future information.

Proponents of this theory point out that it is his disappearance without trace that strengthens this narrative. For them, the absence of any clue to his whereabouts after his release suggests that he was not linked to this time at all. If Carlssin had told the truth about his origin, then his return to the future would explain why he has not been seen since.

The possibility that Carlssin really did time travel opens the door to discussions about scientific theories such as wormholes, relativity and time paradoxes. Science has not yet conclusively proven that time travel is possible, but the theories of quantum physics and general relativity leave room for speculation. In particular, the concept of wormholes, tunnels in space-time, has been explored as a possible way to travel from one point in time to another, though so far only in theory.

Of course, there is no conclusive evidence that time travel is possible. But in the absence of evidence, the mystery remains as fascinating as when it first emerged. In the world of conspiracy theorists and science fiction enthusiasts, Carlssin's story has gained a place alongside other modern legends of time travellers, such as John Titor.

Lack of evidence: the enigma lives on

What is truly intriguing is the lack of conclusive evidence to either prove or disprove the existence of Andrew Carlssin. There are no verifiable records of his arrest, nor of his release on bail, nor of his disappearance. Yet the story lives on in popular culture, resurfacing from time to time in blogs, internet forums and tabloid media as one of the great unsolved mysteries of the financial world.

The Carlssin case represents a crossroads between reality and fantasy, where the line between the two becomes blurred. Is it possible that, in some dark corner of time, Carlssin has returned to his time, with his secret intact? Or are we dealing with one of the most elaborate frauds in recent history, wrapped in a myth that refuses to go away?

Whatever the truth, the enigma continues to capture the imagination of all those who, fascinated by the inexplicable, seek answers in the impossible.

Speculation as to why Carlssin chose to disappear

One intriguing theory that has gained traction is the idea that Carlssin may have planned his own demise, regardless of whether he was a con man, a technological genius or a time traveller. This speculation suggests that Carlssin, realising the media and governmental attention he was attracting, decided to flee for strategic reasons.

Those who defend this theory argue that his disappearance may have been a calculated tactic to protect his identity and keep the mystery alive. Had Carlssin revealed the source of his success or the tools he used, he would have faced serious consequences, legal or otherwise. Fleeing, then, allowed him not only to avoid prosecution, but also to keep the intrigue surrounding his case intact.

Another version of this speculation suggests that he was "eliminated" or silenced by actors who did not want his secrets known. If Carlssin really did have access to advanced technology, insider information or even knowledge of the future, his disappearance may have been facilitated or forced by those who feared this knowledge would fall into the wrong hands. This possibility adds an even more sinister dimension to the Carlssin mystery, suggesting that his disappearance was no mere coincidence, but the result of a larger operation.

Theory of the creation of a "financial legend".

One intriguing theory that has emerged is the possibility that Andrew Carlssin deliberately created his own legend, carefully fabricating the key elements of his story to perpetuate the mystery surrounding him. This theory holds that Carlssin may have used the narrative of being a time traveller, or possessing extraordinary market knowledge, as a calculated strategy to divert attention from his true intentions.

If Carlssin really was a master of financial fraud or a sophisticated con man, the creation of a myth about his ability to predict the future would have served as a perfect smokescreen. By fuelling rumours of his financial immortality, or even his connection to the future, it would have protected his image against more mundane accusations, such as insider trading or market manipulation.

The rumours that began to circulate about his alleged ability to foresee financial movements may have been strategically planted by Carlssin himself. By creating such a fantastic story involving time travel, he would have diverted attention from a more serious investigation and focused on speculation that, by its very nature, is impossible to prove. This strategy, if true, would have helped Carlssin buy time, create confusion and, ultimately, disappear without a trace.

Carlssin's story became bigger than the man himself. By building a myth around himself, he managed to transcend the boundaries of financial logic and entered the realm of modern legend. If this theory is true, Carlssin was not only a brilliant investor or con man, but also a master at manipulating public perception. He knew that the mystery he left behind would be harder to dismantle than any rational explanation of his investments.

This strategy of "creating a legend" may have been his master plan all along: to raise his profile to such an extent that even a well-executed disappearance would be shrouded in speculation, allowing him to remain in the shadows while the world continued to debate his existence.

Chapter 6: Håkan Nordkvist: The Man Who Met His Future Self

In the vast and enigmatic field of time travel stories, Håkan Nordkvist's story stands out as one of the simplest, yet most intriguing cases. Unlike other accounts filled with catastrophic predictions or apocalyptic warnings, Nordkvist's experience was not intended to change the course of humanity or prevent an impending disaster. Instead, his account offers a deeply personal encounter: a meeting with a future version of himself.

Nordkvist's story, which originated in Sweden, caught the attention of the curious in 2006, when he claimed to have accidentally encountered his future self while performing a routine home repair. With no great pretense or hidden messages, Nordkvist shared his story with a mixture of awe and humility, accompanying his testimony with a photograph purportedly capturing this bizarre moment.

What makes his account all the more captivating is the lack of any intention to prove anything extraordinary. There were no warnings, no profound revelations about the fate of humanity, just the simple statement that, for a brief moment, Håkan Nordkvist had the opportunity to see himself several years in the future. However, this element of simplicity and ordinariness, rather than weakening his story, has strengthened it in mystery enthusiast circles. The normality of his account, wrapped in the extraordinary, has made his experience a subject of fascination.

As Nordkvist's account began to spread across the internet, questions arose about its veracity: how is it possible that someone, with no scientific explanation, could find a future version of himself by making a simple repair to the sink in his home? In a world full of theories about wormholes, parallel dimensions and unexplained phenomena, is it plausible that this ordinary man accidentally stumbled into the future?

Moreover, Nordkvist's lack of personal promotion has given his story an aura of authenticity that has been difficult to refute. Unlike other alleged time travellers who have parlayed their tales into fame or fortune, Nordkvist did not seek media attention or attempt to profit from his experience. This humble approach has led some to consider the possibility that his story may not have been fabricated to gain notoriety, but may have been a genuine, if incomprehensible, experience.

Throughout this chapter, we will explore the details of his story, from the accident that led to this unusual encounter, to the controversy over the authenticity of the photo that has come under scrutiny. Finally, we will reflect on the nature of his account: is it just a personal story, or could there be something more behind this mysterious event?

6.1 The accident that led him to meet with his older version

On 30 August 2006, Håkan Nordkvist, an ordinary Swedish man, had an experience that defies logic and the laws of physics as we know them. His account begins mundanely enough, with a plumbing problem in his home, but quickly becomes one of the most intriguing accounts of the supposed interplay between present and future.

On his way home from work that day, Nordkvist discovered that the dishwasher in his house was leaking. As anyone would do, he reached for his tools and set out to fix the problem himself. In retrospect, this event might seem insignificant, but according to him, it was the starting point for something much bigger.

While trying to repair the leak, he noticed something strange: the space under the sink, which should have been limited and narrow, was unusually extended. "It looked like there was more space than usual," Nordkvist later recounted. Intrigued by what was happening, he reached deeper under the sink, only to feel the space around him change. What should have been a confined area was inexplicably lengthening, as if he was entering a kind of tunnel.

Nordkvist described this passage as "distorted" and "shimmering", as if time and space were stretching around him. Although the details of this particular tunnel are unclear, he claimed to have felt that his perception of time was altered, as if he was crossing an invisible barrier.

The next thing he remembers is emerging in a completely different place. The feeling of having left his home and, in a way, his own time, was disconcerting. What struck him most, however, was not the environment he found himself in, but the figure standing in front of him.

There, standing there, was an older version of himself. Although more wrinkled, with visibly greyer hair, this older man's features were unmistakably his own. At first, there was total disbelief. How was this possible? Nordkvist remembered feeling a sense of strangeness, as if he were dreaming or trapped in some kind of illusion.

However, that initial disbelief gave way to the astonishing certainty that he was indeed in front of his future self. The two began to talk, and as they shared memories and personal details that only Nordkvist knew, confirmation came. "He knew things that only I could know," Nordkvist later explained, convinced of the authenticity of his experience.

This encounter, which could have lasted a few minutes or perhaps hours (Nordkvist himself was not sure), was so striking that they decided to document it somehow. The older man, who was himself in the future, and his younger version took a photo together as proof of the encounter. According to Nordkvist, this encounter not only changed his perspective on life, but also challenged everything he thought possible about time and space.

Reflections on the experience and possible interpretations

This account, though extraordinary, has raised many questions among those who have analysed it. What really happened under Håkan Nordkvist's sink? One possibility is that Nordkvist experienced some kind of psychological phenomenon, such as a lucid dream or an out-of-body experience, which could explain the feeling of having passed through a "glowing tunnel" and the encounter with a larger version of himself. In this case, the account would be more a projection of his mind than a physical event.

Another possibility is that Nordkvist has unwittingly entered into a quantum or temporal phenomenon that defies our current understanding of reality. The idea of a tunnel connecting different points in time is common in wormhole theories, although such ideas are purely speculative in modern physics. Still, Nordkvist's description of a distorted passage seems to be in line with theories suggesting the existence of "bridges" between different points in time.

There is also the possibility that this story is part of a narrative created by Nordkvist to convey some kind of philosophical or reflective message about the passage of time and the inevitability of ageing. The story could be a way of confronting fears of what the future holds, and the photo a symbol of reconciliation between the present and what is to come.

The emotional and psychological impact of the encounter

Beyond the nature of the event itself, what is undeniable is the emotional impact it had on Nordkvist. Encountering a future version of oneself could generate a range of complex emotions: from astonishment and disbelief to acceptance and, perhaps, resignation. By his own account, this experience was not frightening, but profoundly revealing. He described feeling an inner peace after his encounter, as if he had somehow received confirmation that his future was secure.

Ultimately, the encounter with his future self offered no great revelations about what was to come, but it did leave Nordkvist with a sense of calm and curiosity. Was it all an illusion, a momentary escape from reality, or proof that time is much more flexible than we think?

6.2 The famous photo and criticisms of its authenticity

The photo that Håkan Nordkvist took with his future version quickly became the subject of fascination and debate on the internet and in circles interested in mysteries and unexplained phenomena. In the image, two men can be seen, one obviously younger than the other, but both with strikingly similar features: similar features, almost identical smiles, and an undeniable familiarity that, to many, seemed to confirm Nordkvist's claim that he had met his future self. For some, this photograph was proof enough to give credence to his account.

However, not everyone was convinced. From the moment the image was shared online, sceptical voices began to analyse it closely. Photo editing experts and digital image analysis enthusiasts pointed to several areas that they felt could indicate digital manipulation. Shadows and lighting were among the most discussed points. It was suggested that the direction and intensity of the shadows did not match what would be expected in an authentic photograph, raising suspicions that the image might have been edited to look more convincing.

In addition to the shadows, some critics also mentioned that the edges of the faces in the photograph showed signs of possible digital overlay. While these criticisms did not conclusively prove that the image was a fake, they did cast doubt on its authenticity. Despite technical analysis, it has never been possible to confirm with certainty whether the image was retouched or altered.

The impact of photography on public perception

Despite criticism and scepticism, the famous photo continued to fuel the mystery surrounding Nordkvist's story. In a world where visual evidence is often seen as the strongest basis for credibility, the existence of this image elevated Nordkvist's story to a whole new level. While many stories of encounters with the future or time travel have no more than oral testimony, the photo provided a tangible anchor that gave his account a level of realism that many other stories lack.

It is interesting to note how the photo was received in different contexts. In some more sceptical circles, it became a symbol of the ease with which images can be manipulated in the digital age. For others, however, the very existence of the image, regardless of whether or not it was manipulated, added a layer of mystery that made the story harder to dismiss. In the internet age, visual evidence, while subject to manipulation, also has significant narrative power. In Nordkvist's case, the photograph was a key element that kept speculation about the veracity of his story alive.

Digital forensics: a possible solution?

With technological advances in digital forensic analysis, it might seem possible that a thorough analysis of the photograph could definitively settle the question of its authenticity. In the years since the image appeared, several enthusiasts have proposed that advanced forensic examination could shed more light on whether the image was tampered with. However, to date, no comprehensive analysis has been carried out that could settle the debate once and for all.

Some experts have suggested that, although today's technology is advanced enough to detect manipulations in digital images, the fact that Nordkvist did not seek official verification may indicate that, for him, the authenticity of the experience is more important than the authenticity of the photo. This position reinforces the idea that Nordkvist was not seeking to convince others, but simply to share what he believed he had experienced.

Nordkvist's scepticism of criticism

One of the most fascinating aspects of Håkan Nordkvist's story is his total disinterest in refuting criticism. In several interviews, Nordkvist stated that he had no need to convince others that his experience was real. For him, the truth of what he experienced was beyond the reach of scientific explanations or public debates. From his perspective, what mattered was what he had experienced, not external validation.

This stance, although it has generated more scepticism among critics, has also served to keep curiosity about his story alive. Unlike other cases of encounters with the future or alleged time travel, Nordkvist never sought to turn his experience into a media phenomenon or to profit from it. This humble approach has led some to consider the possibility that, perhaps, his account was not invented to gain notoriety, but was the result of a deeply personal, authentic, if incomprehensible, experience.

The power of mystery: the photo in the digital age

With the rise of social media and the ability to share content instantly, Håkan Nordkvist's photo has been the subject of countless discussions on mystery forums and platforms. The image is often reused in discussions about time travel, and its popularity has ensured that Nordkvist's story remains part of the collective imagination of the unexplained.

The digital age has made it possible for stories like Nordkvist's to stay alive and evolve over time. Although the image has never been confirmed or denied, the debate surrounding its authenticity is a reflection of how visual evidence plays a central role in the way people perceive reality. In this sense, the famous photo has transcended its original purpose and has become a symbol of the mystery and ambiguity surrounding accounts of encounters with the future.

Final reflections:

Although Håkan Nordkvist's famous photo has never been corroborated as authentic, it remains one of the pillars supporting his story. For those who want to believe in the possibility of time travel, the photo is a fascinating piece of evidence that invites reflection and debate. For sceptics, it is one more image in a long line of possible digital manipulations. What is indisputable is that the photo has managed to keep Nordkvist's story alive, becoming a starting point for deeper questions about the nature of time, perception and reality.

6.3 Personal story or a vision of the future?

Håkan Nordkvist's account raises a fascinating question that has puzzled many: was he simply a personal account of a strange experience, or did he somehow actually witness an encounter with the future? Unlike other cases of alleged time travellers, Nordkvist's story includes no catastrophic warnings, no claims about how to change humanity's destiny. There were no predictions about technological breakthroughs or revelations about important future events. Instead, what Nordkvist offers is a simple story: a brief conversation between two versions of himself.

This simplicity is precisely what makes his story so intriguing. In a world where time travel stories often involve grandiose scenarios or global disasters, Nordkvist's case seems remarkably ordinary, but at the same time extraordinary in its simplicity. There are no dramatic elements; just a conversation between a man and his older version. This raises the question: can such a basic experience be enough to be considered evidence of time travel?

Psychological theories: wishful thinking or lucid dreaming?

One possible explanation that many have put forward is that Nordkvist's experience was the product of an illusion or an altered state of consciousness, such as a lucid dream. In this type of experience, people are able to interact with their environment in a conscious way, even though they are in a state of sleep or semi-sleep. The line between what is real and what is a construct of the mind becomes blurred, which might explain why Nordkvist felt he was in a tunnel and had emerged in another time.

The concept of a "lucid dream" or out-of-body experience has been documented in psychological and neurological studies. During these experiences, people may feel that they are in control of their environment, even though they are in a dreamlike state. This may explain the encounter with a future version of themselves: a reflection of their subconscious, confronting the inevitable passage of time and the anticipation of their ageing.

The idea of Nordkvist projecting his future self into a dream experience also has a symbolic dimension. The conversation with an older version of himself could have been a manifestation of his own fear or curiosity about the future. In many cultures and traditions, the future is seen as a reflection of present decisions, and this encounter could have been a way in which Nordkvist subconsciously processed his relationship to time and ageing.

A philosophical tale: the encounter with oneself

Beyond psychological explanations, we can also interpret Håkan Nordkvist's case from a philosophical perspective. Throughout history, many philosophical currents have explored the concept of the "self" and how it relates to time. In Nordkvist's story, we can see a kind of metaphor for the inevitability of ageing and the continuity of personal identity over time.

Since ancient Greece, philosophers have debated the nature of time and the self. Plato, for example, argued that time is an illusion created by our limited perception. In this sense, Nordkvist's encounter with his future self could be interpreted as a reminder that time, as we perceive it, is simply a construct of our minds, and that the future and the present are much more connected than we think.

The notion of the "future self" may also reflect a Buddhist idea, which holds that the self is not a fixed entity, but a constantly changing series of events and experiences. The fact that Nordkvist has interacted with a larger version of himself may symbolise a view of life as a continuous flow, where the future is not a separate destiny, but a natural extension of the present.

Science and time travel: is it possible?

Although psychological and philosophical explanations offer an interesting way to interpret Nordkvist's account, we cannot ignore the question of whether this case could somehow be a true time travel experience. Although science has not yet conclusively proven that time travel is possible, several theories within modern physics leave room for speculation.

One of the most popular theories of time travel is that of wormholes, hypothetical tunnels in space-time that could connect different points in the universe. Although these wormholes exist only in the realm of mathematical theory, some scientists believe that, if they could be found or created, they could be used for time travel. Is it possible that Nordkvist has inadvertently found a way to access one of these wormholes and, for a brief moment, crossed the barrier between the present and the future?

Another theory that could explain Nordkvist's account is that of "parallel universes". This theory suggests that there are multiple versions of the universe, and that each decision we make creates a new timeline. If this is the case, it is possible that Nordkvist did not travel to the future of his own universe, but to an alternative version where his older self existed at the time. Although these theories are speculative, they provide an interesting framework for interpreting stories such as Nordkvist's.

Cultural impact and legacy of the story

Although Nordkvist's account has been debunked by many as a fantasy or hoax, his story remains a recurring theme among mystery and time travel enthusiasts. The simplicity of his account, coupled with the lack of conclusive evidence to support or refute it, has kept the fascination surrounding his experience alive.

In the cultural context, Nordkvist's story can be seen as part of a wider tradition of tales about time and identity. From literature to film, the theme of time travel has captured the imagination of people all over the world. Stories like Nordkvist's continue to resonate because, at their core, they touch on universal themes: the desire to understand the future, the confrontation with ageing and the search for answers to existential questions.

Chapter 7: Bryant Johnson: The Drunkard from the Future Who Wanted to Warn Us

Tales of time travellers often take a variety of forms, from detailed prophecies to cryptic warnings, and some of them seem to be taken more seriously than others. The case of Bryant Johnson is certainly one of the most peculiar and, for many, one of the hardest to take seriously. In 2017, in the quiet town of Casper, Wyoming, a seemingly ordinary man was arrested by police for being under the influence of alcohol. What began as an ordinary incident in which an intoxicated person was causing trouble, turned into an extraordinary story when Johnson proclaimed that he was not just any drunk, but a time traveller.

Claiming to have arrived from the year 2048, Bryant Johnson claimed that he had been sent back in time to warn humanity of an impending alien invasion. According to his account, the aliens were preparing a massive offensive, and his mission was to alert the population to be prepared. However, his trip had not gone as planned. Johnson explained that he should have arrived in 2018, but due to a technical error, he appeared in 2017, a year ahead of schedule.

What is most curious about his account is that, despite the fantastic nature of his warning, Johnson was evidently intoxicated. He insisted that the aliens had given him large quantities of alcohol to facilitate his time travel, which he claimed explained his state at the time of his arrest. This detail, while absurd to most, added a surreal touch to his story, and soon went viral on social networks and local media.

But beyond the colourfulness of his tale, Johnson's story raises interesting questions about how we react to stories of time travellers, especially when they don't live up to the image we usually have of them. While other time-traveller stories are full of detailed predictions or warnings about the fate of humanity, Johnson's seems more like an incoherent rant. However, as in many other cases of time travellers, it is this mixture of the absurd and the extraordinary that keeps the audience's fascination alive.

This case also offers a reflection on how apocalyptic warnings, even when they come from unreliable sources, can capture people's attention.

In an era marked by uncertainty about the future, the idea of an alien invasion or any other catastrophic event remains a recurring theme, and people are willing to pay attention, if only to mock or debate the veracity of these claims.

In this chapter, we explore Bryant Johnson's warning, the reaction it generated among authorities and the public, and what this story reveals about our continuing fascination with time travellers, apocalyptic prophets and the future of humanity.

7.1 The warning of an alien invasion

During his arrest, Bryant Johnson surprised officials by claiming that he was not only a time traveller, but that he had been sent from the year 2048 on a crucial mission: to warn humanity of an impending alien invasion. According to his account, extraterrestrial forces were preparing to launch a massive attack on Earth, an event that would threaten the survival of humanity as we know it.

The curious thing about his warning is that, despite being in an obvious state of inebriation, Johnson insisted that his state was not the result of irresponsible behaviour, but part of the process that had led him to time travel. He explained that the aliens had given him large quantities of alcohol to prepare him for time travel, a method that, while bizarre, was a fundamental part of the technology the aliens used to manipulate time.

The symbolism of an alien invasion

The warning of an alien invasion, though absurd to many, is not a new idea in popular culture. Since the earliest days of science fiction, stories of alien invasion have captured people's imaginations, in many cases reflecting contemporary fears and uncertainties. In the case of Bryant Johnson, his warning of an impending invasion could be interpreted as a manifestation of those same fears, amplified by his altered mental state.

In the context of his account, aliens represent not only an external threat, but also a symbol of the unknown, of forces beyond our control that could radically alter the way we live. In a world where conspiracy theories about UFOs and extraterrestrial life have been the subject of fascination for decades, Johnson's warning fits within a broader tradition of apocalyptic prophecies in which alien forces are seen as an existential threat.

Time travel: forced or voluntary?

One of Johnson's most intriguing claims was that his time travel was not voluntary. According to his account, he was "forced" to travel back in time by the aliens themselves, who wanted him to be the messenger to warn humanity. This detail introduces an interesting dynamic into Johnson's narrative: he was not a willing hero, but someone caught up in an alien plan much bigger than himself.

This concept of being "forced" to travel through time by a superior force adds a layer of intrigue to the story. The idea that alien beings could manipulate time and use humans as pawns in their plans for the future suggests a dystopian vision, where humanity has no control over its destiny and is at the mercy of more powerful forces. While Johnson did not provide many details about how this technology worked or why he was chosen, his account touches on themes that resonate with the stories of alien control and temporal manipulation present in numerous science fiction narratives.

The accidental arrival of the year 2017

Another peculiar aspect of Johnson's warning is that, according to him, the time travel did not go as planned. Instead of arriving in 2018, as had been his original intention, it appeared in 2017 due to a "technical error". This part of the story adds a component of chaos and randomness to his narrative, which could be interpreted in several ways. On the one hand, it could be seen as a way to justify the inconsistencies in his story; on the other hand, it could reflect the idea that even when it comes to advanced technology, human (or alien, in this case) mistakes are still inevitable.

Johnson's accidental arrival in the wrong year also introduces an interesting paradox: if his mission was to warn humanity in 2018, did he change anything by appearing a year earlier? Such temporal dilemmas are common in time travel stories, where small changes in the past can have unpredictable consequences in the future. However, Johnson does not seem to have worried too much about the implications of having arrived too early, focusing more on the urgency of his message.

Lack of details on the invasion

One notable aspect of Johnson's warning is the lack of specific details about the alien invasion. Despite his assertions about the imminent threat, he did not offer clear information about when or how the invasion would occur, nor did he give details about the nature of the alien creatures or their technology. This gap in his account could be due to his state of mind at the time, but it could also be interpreted as part of the symbolism of apocalyptic warnings in general.

Apocalyptic warnings often lack precise details, allowing the fear of disaster to be amplified as the mind fills in the gaps with its own anxieties. In Johnson's case, the lack of detail may have served to make his warning more frightening to those willing to consider it. By not offering a specific date or a clear description of the invaders, his account remains in the realm of uncertainty, fuelling speculation rather than providing clear answers.

Receipt of your warning

Despite his inebriated state and widespread disbelief, Johnson's warning of alien invasion did not go unnoticed. In the days following his arrest, the story went viral, capturing the attention of both serious media and entertainment platforms. While most people dismissed it as an alcohol-induced fantasy, some conspiracy theorists began to discuss the possibility that Johnson may have been telling the truth.

This phenomenon is not uncommon in contemporary culture. Apocalyptic warnings, whether about aliens, natural disasters or government conspiracies, have a special appeal to certain groups, especially those already suspicious of official narratives. In Johnson's case, his warning, though unclear, fit a familiar pattern of prophecies about the end of the world and the role of the "chosen ones" who are sent to warn humanity.

7.2 Police reaction and public disbelief

When Casper police arrested Bryant Johnson, they found him in an obviously intoxicated state. According to police reports, Johnson had difficulty standing and his speech was incoherent at several points. However, in the midst of his confusion, he was surprisingly clear in insisting that he was not just a random drunk, but a time traveller sent from the year 2048 to warn of an impending alien invasion. To the arresting officers, his intoxicated state was enough to quickly dismiss his account as a simple alcohol-induced hallucination.

The authorities' initial response

Casper police treated Johnson as they would any other intoxicated individual: they detained him to ensure his safety and the safety of others.

What distinguished this case, however, was Johnson's insistence that he must communicate with "higher authorities". According to his claims, the fate of humanity was at stake, and he needed to alert the most powerful figures to take immediate action against the impending alien invasion.

The police report records the disbelief of the officers. Although they attempted to reason with him and obtain clearer details about his warning, the coherence in his account fell apart as he spoke. The combination of his mental state and his lack of clarity caused the officers to understandably dismiss his account as a product of his inebriation. This kind of reaction by authorities is common when confronted with extraordinary stories told by people in altered states of consciousness. The police, accustomed to dealing with unusual situations, would probably have treated the case as just another incident of people under the influence of alcohol.

Public disbelief and widespread scepticism

When details of Johnson's arrest became public and the story was covered by the media, the case quickly became a source of ridicule and ironic commentary. Sensationalist headlines referring to him as the "drunkard of the future" soon generated immediate reactions on social media. Memes and satirical comments quickly spread, and Johnson's story became another case demonstrating how public disbelief can be both cruel and immediate when someone presents a narrative that defies logic or common sense.

However, behind the initial reaction of disbelief, there also emerged a small but vocal group of people who saw Johnson's account as more than just drunkenness. For some conspiracy theorists, the incident was taken as an example of how important warnings can be ridiculed and dismissed to prevent people from taking them seriously. According to these believers, the reaction of the media and the police was a deliberate attempt to hide the truth behind a "cloak of humour". In their view, Johnson's story could be a legitimate warning that was distorted to avoid widespread panic.

This type of response is not new. Throughout history, there have been cases where seemingly deranged individuals have made outlandish claims, only to be ignored by the majority. In many of these cases, the figure of the "prophetic madman" has been used to ridicule those who claim to have information about the future or apocalyptic events. The public response to Johnson's story, then, follows a familiar pattern: a mixture of disbelief, derision and a small fraction of people who cling to the possibility that the message, however bizarre, might have an underlying truth.

Social media as a catalyst for the viral phenomenon

One of the reasons Bryant Johnson's story went viral so quickly was the ability of social media to amplify unusual accounts. Within hours, his story was shared, commented on and reinterpreted by thousands of people on platforms such as Twitter, Facebook and Reddit. Social media, with its ability to transform any curious tale into a viral phenomenon, played a crucial role in the rapid spread of Johnson's case.

In a world where the immediacy of information can be both a blessing and a curse, social media not only amplifies stories like Johnson's, but also allows people to take different positions: from mockery and scepticism to passionate defence of conspiracy theories. Digital platforms have facilitated the creation of communities that are willing to discuss any topic, no matter how improbable, and Johnson's case was no exception.

We might consider that the viralization of Johnson's story also reflects the collective desire to find humour and entertainment in unusual situations, while at the same time, some people seek meaning in the extraordinary. This phenomenon is not unique to social media, but these platforms have accelerated its spread and amplified its cultural impact. What could have been simply a colourful blurb on the local news in Casper was transformed, thanks to the power of the internet, into a global phenomenon that was discussed all over the world.

Institutional and cultural scepticism

The disbelief of the police and the general public at Johnson's account can also be interpreted as part of a wider cultural scepticism towards any narrative that challenges the logical order of the world. We live in an era where, despite the fascination with conspiracy theories and supernatural phenomena, institutions and most people continue to rely on tangible evidence and reason. In this context, Johnson's claims of time travel and alien invasion lacked any evidence that could be taken seriously.

Johnson's case highlights how extraordinary stories, especially when they come from individuals in compromising situations, are often dismissed without further analysis. Unlike other more elaborate accounts of time travel, Johnson did not offer detailed predictions or show any special knowledge that could support his claim. This, coupled with his mental state at the time of his arrest, meant that the police and the public gave him no more credence than a drunk could receive.

7.3 What does this story tell us about the belief in time travellers?

Bryant Johnson's story, though initially ridiculed, offers a fascinating insight into how the public and institutions react to the claims of supposed time travellers. Throughout history, accounts of people claiming to have travelled through time have ranged from outright scepticism to outright fascination. Johnson's case shows how these stories, however improbable they may seem, continue to capture people's imagination.

First, this case reveals a recurring trend: apocalyptic warnings. Whether it is prophecies about the end of the world, alien invasions or climate catastrophes, warnings from people who claim to have seen the future are a common theme in time traveller stories. These warnings often reflect contemporary societal fears. In Johnson's case, his warning of an alien invasion can be seen as a manifestation of modern fears about technology, alien control, or even government surveillance and control.

On the other hand, we also see how Johnson's intoxication served to delegitimise his account from the outset. In many other cases of alleged time travellers, individuals who make such claims are often dismissed as "unbalanced" or "liars", and the evidence against them - or lack thereof - reinforces this disbelief. Johnson's story highlights how public perception of a person's sanity greatly affects how their message is received, even if that message has intriguing elements or is consistent with popular theories.

Finally, the case of Bryant Johnson highlights the public's continuing fascination with stories about time travellers. Although his account was ridiculed by most, there remains a small segment of the population that is willing to consider the possibility that some of these warnings, however far-fetched they may seem, may have an element of truth to them. In a world filled with uncertainty and fears about the future, time-traveller stories like Johnson's offer a window into our own anxieties about what might lie ahead.

The need to believe in the extraordinary: The case of Bryant Johnson highlights a human tendency towards belief in the unbelievable, especially in times of uncertainty or social instability. The story of a time traveller warning of an alien invasion may seem absurd to many, but to others, it fits into a broader pattern of apocalyptic theories and extraordinary events. This desire to believe in the supernatural or in the intervention of outside forces can be interpreted as a psychological response to the lack of control over the future or the uncertainty of everyday life.

In times of crisis, stories about apocalyptic warnings tend to gain traction. Tales of time travellers warning of impending catastrophe resonate because they play on widespread anxiety about the fragility of the world and uncertainty about what might happen. In Johnson's case, his warning about an alien invasion reflects this same kind of fear. No matter how ridiculous the story may seem to some, there are those who find comfort in the possibility that there is someone with knowledge of the future who can warn of what is to come.

The psychological appeal of false prophets: These figures often emerge in times of crisis or uncertainty, when people seek answers about the future. Although Johnson did not present himself as a prophet in the traditional sense, his warning about an alien invasion has certain parallels with the messages of false prophets, who often foresee catastrophes. Such warnings, however implausible, offer some people a sense of order or purpose in the face of uncertainty.

When societies face economic crises, political tensions or natural disasters, widespread uncertainty leads many to seek an explanation or a vision of the future that provides meaning and security. False prophet figures, who bring with them warnings of impending disaster, often attract followers because they offer a narrative that appears to structure chaos. In this context, Johnson, while not identifying himself as a prophet, captured the imagination of some people who may have sought to find some kind of meaning in his warning of an alien invasion, even if most dismissed it as fantasy.

The entertainment factor in virality: In the age of the internet and social media, implausible stories like Johnson's tend to go viral quickly. This phenomenon speaks to a culture where the fine line between truth and fiction is often blurred, and entertainment sometimes takes precedence over fact. Bryant Johnson's story, like many others about alleged time travellers, was not only ridiculed, but also widely shared and commented on, helping to keep public curiosity alive.

Through social media, stories that would otherwise have been confined to small circles of interest are amplified, often without deep critical evaluation. Entertainment takes over, and Johnson's story is transformed into a 'viral event', where the absurd and bizarre become topics of conversation, memes and commentary. This also highlights a tendency to trivialise or treat extraordinary stories as passing entertainment, rather than analysing them in depth, leading to an oversimplification of the subject matter.

The phenomenon of conspiracy as a psychological refuge: Tales of time travellers are often linked to conspiracy theories, where institutions or governments are seen as hiding deeper 'truths'. In the case of Bryant Johnson, some conspiracy theorists argued that his arrest and subsequent public ridicule were part of a larger effort to silence someone who knew too much. Such narratives feed a widespread perception of distrust of the authorities and the official media.

This aspect can be seen in a broader context of social mistrust. People who believe in conspiracy theories often seek alternative explanations to official narratives, and alleged time travellers fit that search. Apocalyptic warnings, however unlikely, provide a structure onto which conspiracy theorists can project their fears and interpretations of the world. In Johnson's case, his warning of an alien invasion fits perfectly into this mould, where distrust of the authorities becomes the basis for interpreting his account as a possible attempt at a cover-up.

The role of alcohol and sanity: Public disbelief of Johnson's claims was primarily linked to his drunkenness at the time of his arrest. However, it also raises questions about how society deals with extraordinary claims made by people who are not considered "credible" or "rational". That is, how many unusual stories are dismissed just because the people telling them do not meet traditional standards of 'sanity' or sobriety?

This point reveals a subtle discrimination in how extraordinary accounts are handled. Claims by intoxicated individuals, or those who are perceived as mentally unstable, tend to be automatically ignored or dismissed. But what happens when these people present a narrative that challenges social norms? You might reflect on how society treats marginalised voices and whether it is possible for some important stories to be dismissed because of public perception of the messenger's mental or physical state.

Chapter 8: William Taylor: The Future Spy Who Visited the Year 8973

The case of William Taylor is particularly interesting because it departs from typical narratives of time travellers who return to the past or travel to times closer to the present. Instead of warning of impending disasters or speaking of predictable technological advances, Taylor claimed to have been sent to the year 8973, a future so distant that humanity, according to him, no longer resembled anything like what we know today.

What makes his story unique is not only the extremely distant temporal destination, but the context in which he claimed to have travelled: an intertemporal espionage mission. According to his account, Taylor was neither an accidental time traveller nor a chance witness to the future, but a trained spy, sent specifically to observe and gather information in this distant future.

Taylor described how social and political structures in the year 8973 had been replaced by an entirely new form of organisation. Technology was the mainstay of civilisation, but unlike our current fears about technological control, in his version of the future, technology had enabled humans to achieve a utopian society, where artificial intelligence and biotechnologies had not only eradicated poverty, but had merged the human with the artificial. At this point, humanity was no longer bound by biological limitations, but had evolved into posthuman forms.

The most striking thing about his account is the way he described control over time and space. Travel was not only possible, but a normal part of everyday life for the inhabitants of the future. This transformed the notion of inter-temporal "espionage" into something more akin to a scientific observation, where the concept of linear time had been superseded.

This point leads us to reflect not only on future technological possibilities, but also on the ethical and philosophical implications of time travel in non-linear contexts. Taylor's story raises important questions about what defines humanity and how, by projecting our current concerns onto distant visions of the future, we construct narratives that reflect both our fears and our aspirations.

8.1 An intertemporal spy's tale: What did he see in the future?

William Taylor claimed that his experience in the year 8973 was something that even the best training as an intertemporal spy could not have prepared him to face. Arriving in that distant future, he found a civilisation so advanced that humanity as we know it seemed to have been completely overtaken. Not just in the technological sense, but in the biological and mental foundations that define what it means to be human.

The disappearance of the human form as we know it

Taylor said that one of the first things he noticed was that the humans of this time did not seem at all human in the traditional sense. They had evolved, or perhaps completely transformed, into a new race of advanced beings. They were tall and slender, with elongated limbs, but what was most striking was the way their bodies seemed to merge with technology.

Biotechnology integration

These beings, according to Taylor, had achieved a complete integration of biology and technology. Every cell in their bodies was optimised by nanotechnology, allowing them to regenerate, control their environment and process information at levels beyond our current understanding. This fusion not only made them physically superior, but also gave them extraordinary mental abilities, such as telepathy and the ability to manipulate their own material environment without the need for external devices. The tools they used were not visible, as the technology had become internalised, part of their very biology.

Moreover, this fusion of the biological and the technological was not only functional, but also rooted in a culture of respect and care for the body as an extension of the mind. Taylor pointed out that the bodies of these beings did not age or experience physical deterioration, as nanotechnological advances allowed for the constant repair of tissues and the seamless maintenance of vital functions.

A world in harmony with nature and technology

What surprised Taylor most was not only the advanced technology, but the symbiosis between it and the natural environment. Instead of dominating nature, as modern humanity has done, the inhabitants of the year 8973 lived in perfect harmony with it. The vast structures Taylor observed, gleaming cities stretching as far as the eye could see, did not interfere with the ecosystem, but seemed to be part of it. The cities floated above the oceans or camouflaged themselves in the forests, absorbing energy directly from the environment without harming it.

This perfect balance between technology and nature was not simply the result of scientific advances, but also reflected a philosophical and spiritual evolution. According to Taylor, the beings of the future had a deep understanding of the connections between all life forms, the planet and the universe, which led them to structure their societies and technologies in such a way that they integrated effortlessly with the natural ecosystem. This collective consciousness was reflected not only in architecture and urban planning, but also in the way they consumed energy and interacted with their environment.

The elimination of ageing and pain

According to Taylor, the concepts of ageing, disease and death had been eradicated millennia ago. The inhabitants of this future did not age, and pain was a completely archaic idea. Through advanced genetic manipulation and the integration of their bodies with nanotechnology, these beings were virtually immortal, although some could choose to "disappear" or transform into new forms of existence whenever they wished. Notions of the human life cycle as we understand it had been completely superseded.

Taylor described how the inhabitants of the year 8973 had reached a state in which personal decisions, even about the end of their physical existence, were completely free. Some chose to live indefinitely, while others chose to experience new forms of existence, unconstrained by the restrictions of the biological body. This ability to choose also affected the way they perceived the passage of time. For these beings, life was not a linear sequence of events, but a fluid experience where chronology could be modified according to their desires.

The society of the year 8973: peace, equality and perfection

Taylor was astonished by the social organisation of this future society. Notions of conflict, war, poverty or inequality had ceased to exist long before his arrival. The inhabitants of the year 8973 lived in a kind of perfect equilibrium, where the material, emotional and intellectual needs of all individuals were effortlessly met.

The end of wars and inequality

Wars, according to Taylor, were an archaic concept that had been forgotten. The civilisation of the future had overcome the divisions that traditionally caused conflict: politics, religion, race and gender no longer existed as sources of discord. Society was organised around principles of equality and cooperation, and there were no visible hierarchies or traditional systems of government. The inhabitants seemed to govern themselves, supported by an artificial intelligence of immense dimensions, which, in Taylor's words, "keeps everything in perfect balance".

Taylor suggested that this artificial intelligence was not oppressive or authoritarian, but acted as an enabler, optimising every aspect of daily life and ensuring that all individuals had access to the same resources and opportunities. This AI was not seen as an external entity, but as an integral part of society, evolved alongside the beings of the future and respected for its ability to maintain collective well-being.

Manipulation of time and space

One of Taylor's most intriguing claims was that the people of 8973 not only mastered their physical environment, but also had total control over time and space. According to Taylor, the notion of time travel or moving across vast spatial distances was an everyday occurrence for this civilisation.

Absolute control of time

In his account, Taylor described how the inhabitants of the future could manipulate time, both individually and collectively. They no longer moved along a strict timeline, as we do; instead, they could move backwards or forwards in time at will, adjusting their experience of the world to suit their needs. Taylor speculated that, thanks to this control over time, beings of this era could live indefinitely without the physical limitations of mortality, returning at specific times to "revisit" experiences or avoid mistakes. This ability, according to Taylor, was the result of an understanding and mastery of the laws of physics that allowed them to interact with space-time in a way that our science cannot yet conceive.

Instant transport

In terms of transport, Taylor claimed that travel from one place to another was instantaneous thanks to a system that transcended our current understanding of physics. It wasn't planes, trains or any other means we can imagine. Rather, it was a kind of quantum teleportation, where bodies and objects were dematerialised at one point and reconstructed at another without delay. This made the concept of distance or boundaries irrelevant to the inhabitants of the future.

Reflections on Taylor's experience

Taylor's account, while fascinating, raises many questions: is it really possible for a human civilisation to achieve such a degree of perfection and control? Taylor described a utopia in which technology and nature were not opposites, but allies. In this world, problems that seem intractable today - such as poverty, wars and physical suffering - had been completely eliminated.

However, the account also leaves room for speculation: was Taylor witnessing a genuine reality or was his experience the result of manipulation or illusion? Furthermore, the claim that these beings possessed such control over time and space introduces a whole new level of complexity: if such mastery is possible, why have they not interacted with us, the humans of the past, in a more direct way?

Ultimately, William Taylor's experience in the year 8973 challenges not only our understanding of what it means to be human, but also the very laws of physics and time. His account, though incredible, continues to resonate with those who believe that the future has the potential to exceed our wildest expectations.

8.2 An unbelievable story without evidence: Media scepticism

As with many of these time-traveller stories, Taylor's claim was met with immediate scepticism, especially due to the lack of evidence. Although his account was full of fascinating details about a future society, he provided no tangible evidence that could corroborate his claims. There were no photographs, artefacts or verifiable records of his alleged journey. This led many, including media and science experts, to dismiss his story as a fantasy or a fabrication intended to attract attention.

The media that covered his story treated it largely as a curiosity, presenting his account more as entertainment than serious news. Criticism soon followed, especially from scientists and experts who pointed out the huge inconsistencies in his account and the technical impossibility of achieving time travel to such a distant time. However, as in other cases of time travellers, a small group of believers stuck to their story, arguing that the lack of evidence does not necessarily discredit their experience, as they could be withholding key information for national security reasons or to protect themselves from reprisals.

Scepticism came not only from the media, but also from the scientific community. Experts pointed out that while the theory of time travel is a topic of debate in theoretical physics, the details of Taylor's account lacked scientific rigour. Descriptions of the technologies and biology of future inhabitants did not align with projections of human evolution or feasible technological models based on current knowledge.

Despite this criticism, Taylor maintained his version of events and claimed that the reasons behind his intertemporal mission were part of a highly confidential programme, which prevented him from revealing certain details that could have lent credibility to his account. This, however, only added to the widespread scepticism, as many people saw this lack of transparency as an attempt to avoid difficult questions about the veracity of his story.

The reaction of the general public

While the media and the scientific community attacked his credibility, Taylor's story did not go unnoticed by the general public. Despite the lack of evidence, his account provoked considerable interest, especially in forums and groups dedicated to conspiracy theories and unsolved mysteries. These audiences saw Taylor's story not just as a passing curiosity, but as a possible preview of a future that most could not imagine.

The general public, at least some of it, was willing to entertain the idea that time travel might be real, and that Taylor might have been a key player in a covert plan of which he could not reveal more details. The possibility of a future as extraordinary as the one Taylor described fascinated many people, who, even if they did not fully believe his story, saw it as a kind of warning or harbinger of the future.

The influence of popular culture and science fiction

The fascination with stories like Taylor's did not arise in a vacuum. The cultural context of the late 20th and early 21st centuries was deeply influenced by science fiction and popular culture, which fuelled the idea of time travel and dystopian futures. Films such as "Terminator", "Back to the Future" and the growing popularity of stories such as John Titor's had prepared the public to accept, or at least consider, narratives involving time travellers.

Taylor fit perfectly into this popular narrative. Although his account lacked evidence, the public had already been exposed to similar ideas through fiction, which made it easy for many to take it seriously, or at least debate it intensely. It was not just a question of whether or not to believe his story; the very idea of time travel was appealing because it touched on some of humanity's deepest desires: control over time and destiny.

Conspiracy theories: Intentional concealment of evidence?

Taylor's failure to provide concrete evidence for his alleged time travel fuelled a number of conspiracy theories. Proponents of his story suggested that the lack of evidence might not be accidental. To them, Taylor might be under surveillance or pressure from government entities or powerful forces that wanted to suppress the truth about time travel. This made his story even more intriguing: if he really had travelled to the future and back, who or what was stopping him from sharing more tangible evidence?

Some theorists argued that Taylor himself may have been protecting himself, avoiding revealing more information for fear of reprisals. These theories speculated about the existence of covert programmes, such as the famous "secret projects" often mentioned in conspiracy theories. In this view, the absence of evidence did not discredit Taylor, but added another layer of mystery that made his account even more attractive to those willing to believe in the possibility of time travel.

The role of collective psychology

Another interesting aspect of the Taylor phenomenon is the role that collective psychology played in the reception of his story. While many people were sceptical, others were willing to believe, or at least to consider the possibility that his story was true. In times of uncertainty, the idea that someone could travel into the future and return with crucial information about the evolution of humanity offered a kind of comfort or hope, even if only as a fantasy.

The belief in time-traveller stories reflects a deep desire to escape from current reality and, in many cases, to get answers to existential questions. The fact that Taylor described such a different future, where the problems plaguing humanity today had been solved, made his story appealing, especially to those who were looking for answers outside conventional paradigms.

Believers and defenders: Could lack of evidence be part of the plan?

Despite widespread scepticism, Taylor found a base of supporters who defended his account. These believers argued that the absence of evidence was, in fact, proof in itself of the veracity of his story. According to them, if Taylor really was part of a secret mission from the future, it was logical that he could not provide direct evidence of his journey, as this could have serious repercussions for his mission and for temporal continuity.

For these advocates, Taylor was not only an intertemporal spy, but also a protector of time and chronological order. His lack of evidence was justified as an act of responsibility, avoiding altering the natural course of history. Moreover, some of his followers speculated that Taylor may have been deliberately ambiguous in order to protect future technology from falling into the wrong hands. Such theories, while difficult to prove, only served to add to the intrigue surrounding his story.

The Shadow of Conspiracy: A Social Experiment?

One of the most interesting theories to emerge around Taylor's story is the possibility that his account was actually a social experiment or a deliberate act of disinformation. Some critics speculated that his story may have been an attempt to study how the public reacts to the possibility of time travel. This theory suggests that Taylor, or whoever was behind his story, wanted to observe how stories that lack tangible evidence, but appeal to the deepest human emotions and hopes, spread and persist.

This idea is not so far-fetched if we consider other cases of false stories that managed to capture the public imagination despite lacking evidence. Taylor's case, according to this theory, could have been a way of measuring the impact of science fiction narratives when presented as fact, or even a way of diverting attention from other more pressing or real issues.

Final reflections: Fact or elaborate fiction?

As time went on, Taylor's story faded from the media spotlight, but not from the minds of those who followed it closely. Lack of evidence, inconsistency in some details, and the general public's growing distrust of time-traveller stories contributed to many viewing it as an elaborate fantasy. However, for his most loyal followers, the absence of evidence was never a decisive factor in dismissing his story.

Ultimately, William Taylor's story remains one of those enigmas that, despite lacking evidence, continues to resonate with those who believe in the possibility of a future where technology has transcended our wildest expectations. And although many dismissed it as an invention, his story lives on in popular culture, fuelling debate and keeping alive the eternal question: is it possible that someone has seen the future and come back to tell the tale?

Chapter 9: Bella: The Woman Who Travelled to the Year 3800

Bella's story is one of those that seems straight out of a science fiction movie, and yet it has captured the attention of many curious people on the internet. A woman from the present who claims to have travelled to the year 3800? It's hard not to be intrigued by the idea. And even more so when Bella didn't just recount her experience in words: according to her, she brought proof. Among her most controversial claims was a photograph, a blurred image she claimed to have taken in the future, surrounded by advanced robots in a fully automated city.

What is fascinating about this story is not only the vision Bella offered of the year 3800, but how she presented it at a time when time travel stories seemed to be all the rage on the internet. Although her account has been called into question and many consider it just another viral theory, there is something about her version that has managed to stick in the minds of those who heard it. Perhaps it is the mystery of what he described: a future where robots not only coexist with humans, but have replaced them in most functions, or perhaps the controversy he stirred up with that famous photograph.

A Future Dominated by Technology

Bella described the year 3800 as a world where humans were no longer the dominant species. In her account, robots were in charge of all important tasks, from city administration to agriculture and industrial production. Humans, those who remained, lived in small communities, isolated from the large metropolises dominated by artificial intelligences.

Interestingly, according to Bella, these robots were not only designed to serve humans; they had evolved to the point of developing a consciousness of their own. They were capable of making complex decisions and, in many cases, acted completely independently. The coexistence between humans and robots in this future was not hostile, but it was marked by a clear separation. Most humans no longer participated in global decision-making, and the robots had assumed that role, not because of a rebellion, but because humans simply ceased to be interested in controlling their own destinies.

Bella recounted how technology was so integrated into everyday life that it was barely noticeable. Floating cities, automated vehicles and self-sufficient factories required no human supervision. For the inhabitants of the year 3800, the idea of "working" or "making decisions" was no longer part of their reality.

The Photograph That Changed Everything

However, what really ignited the debate around Bella was the image she brought with her. It was a blurry, poorly lit photograph, but one in which she claimed to be standing next to a group of robots from the future. In the image, there was a human figure that Bella identified as herself, surrounded by shadows that she said were the advanced robots she described. The image was posted on several forums, and as expected, criticism was quick to follow. Many branded it a fake, pointing out that it looked like a poorly staged montage, while others claimed it was simply too good to be true.

But Bella defended the authenticity of the photograph, explaining that the shooting conditions were difficult due to the time-capture technology he was using. According to her version, the technology that enabled time travel also affected the quality of the images and objects that could be transported back to the present. And while this explanation did not convince the majority, there was a small group of supporters who believed his account, arguing that while the image was not clear, it might be the only possible visual evidence of real time travel.

The Impact on Digital Culture

The truth is that, beyond the authenticity of the photograph or the veracity of the story, Bella's story appeared at a key moment: when the internet was full of viral stories about time travellers, artificial intelligences and conspiracy theories. And her story did not go unnoticed. The idea of a future controlled by robots was not new, but what made her story stand out was the combination of elements: a supposedly ordinary woman claiming to have been part of a secret time travel experiment, and an image that promised to be "proof" of the future.

As her story spread across forums and social media, Bella became a controversial figure. Some saw her as a phony who was taking advantage of the rise of viral stories to gain notoriety, while others saw her as a possible messenger of an unsettling future. In a world where artificial intelligences are beginning to play an increasingly important role, the idea that in the year 3800 robots may have taken over doesn't seem so far-fetched, does it?

In any case, Bella's story remains one of those tales that, despite criticism and doubts, continues to fuel the collective imagination about what the future might hold. Could it be possible that Bella really has seen what is to come? While her photography may not convince everyone, the intrigue and mystery surrounding her story ensures that it will remain alive in discussions about the future and time travel.

9.1 Robots and photos of the future: The story behind Bella

Bella appeared on the scene almost unexpectedly, when on an internet forum she shared what she described as "evidence" of her time travel to the year 3800. According to her account, she was selected as part of a secret government experiment involving time travel. She claims to have been transported to a distant future where humanity has been replaced by a society of advanced robots. In her descriptions, Bella details fully automated futuristic cities where humans, as we know them today, barely existed.

The Context of the Experiment: Why Bella?

One of the biggest unknowns in her story was the motive behind her selection to participate in such a momentous project. Why her? Bella hinted that it was not an accident, but that she had been chosen specifically for skills or characteristics that she did not fully disclose. This added to the atmosphere of mystery surrounding her story. She also mentioned that the experiment was part of a larger operation, orchestrated by government entities, suggesting a level of secrecy and organisation that will probably never be revealed to the public.

Bella hinted that she was not the only one on this trip, which opened the door to the possibility that there was a larger team, with different missions. This small group would have been sent to observe and document key aspects of the future, which would explain her insistence that the image she brought back, though blurred, was a legitimate attempt to provide evidence.

The Journey Process: Unsettling Technology

According to Bella, time travel was not exactly as it is shown in the movies. It was not simply a matter of stepping into a machine and appearing in another time. Instead, she described a much more complex process, almost as if her body had been "dematerialised" and reconstituted in the year 3800. This experience, she said, left temporary physical after-effects after her return, mentioning that, for a time, she felt strange, as if her body had undergone imperceptible changes. Although she offered no direct evidence of this discomfort, this part of her account raised more questions than it answered.

This aspect of the journey may also explain the difficulties he faced in trying to capture tangible evidence. The technology he used, while advanced, was far from perfect for bringing back clear objects or images from the future without them suffering some kind of distortion on the way back.

The Robotic Society: Inevitable Future?

Bella not only described a future filled with robots, she spoke of a civilisation dominated by them. Large cities were fully automated, run by artificial intelligences that were not only more efficient than humans, but had surpassed humanity in ethical and moral capacity. This robotic government was neither oppressive nor tyrannical; on the contrary, Bella claimed that the robots treated humans with respect, seeing them as a fragile species to be protected.

The remaining humans lived in small communities far from the big cities, in a peaceful coexistence, but clearly subordinated to the decisions made by the machines. Humanity had decided, according to Bella, to relinquish control of key decisions, relying on robotic intelligences to manage global welfare. This was a world where human ambition had been replaced by robotic efficiency, and according to her account, this was not something imposed by force, but by humanity's conscious choice to live without conflict.

Robots with Conscience: Advanced Ethics

Bella revealed that these robots were not simply highly logical machines, but had developed a deep understanding of ethical principles. Not only could they make data-driven decisions; they understood the impacts of their actions on an emotional and moral level, making them compassionate stewards of a world where nature and technology coexisted in perfect harmony. This notion was difficult for many to accept, as it raises the possibility that an artificial intelligence could somehow develop what we perceive as emotions or a moral conscience.

Robots did not treat humans as inferior; rather, they saw humans as an important part of the ecosystem, something to be preserved and respected. This was a vision of the future that was the complete opposite of classic narratives of robotic rebellions or technological dystopias. For Bella, robots had achieved what humanity could not: to build a world based on solid ethical principles, where the survival and well-being of all living beings was a priority.

The Technological-Natural Balance

Bella also described a future in which technology and nature were no longer opposing forces. Robots not only ruled cities; they also ensured that the planet was kept in balance. Cities floated on oceans, forests were an integral part of cities, and energy came from renewable sources that did not harm the environment. This was not a future of polluting factories or overexploitation of resources, but of a seamless integration between the artificial and the natural.

This balance, according to Bella, had been made possible by robotic decisions that eliminated the inequalities and conflicts typical of humanity. While humans lived in peace, the robots ensured that the planet would never again experience the damage caused by the bad decisions of human governments or corporations.

Photography: The Controversial Evidence

One of the most intriguing aspects of her story was the alleged photographic evidence she presented. In a blurred image, Bella showed what she claimed was a selfie taken in the future, showing her accompanied by what she described as "a robotic intelligence". The image, although of low quality, showed humanoid figures with advanced features, such as metallic skin and eyes that emitted a blue glow.

The photograph quickly became the focus of debate. Bella explained that the image distortion was due to the unique conditions of time travel. The time jump affected cameras and other devices, preventing them from capturing clear images. While this explanation was not enough to convince sceptics, some argued that, if time travel really was possible, it would be logical that physical interference would affect evidence that could be brought back.

The fact that the image was blurred only added to the mystery. While some considered it to be a simple montage, others argued that the image's imperfections could be an indication of its authenticity. Bella's photograph was not what everyone expected as proof of future travel, but in a sense, precisely its lack of clarity made it a symbol for those who wanted to believe in the possibility of time travel.

What if Bella Was Right?

Bella's account raises an unsettling question: what if she was telling the truth? While the lack of tangible evidence and the controversy surrounding the photograph leaves many doubts, the possibility of a future where robots take control and rule more ethically than humans does not seem so far-fetched. According to his account, these robots did not subjugate humanity, but rather, in their infinite logical and moral capacity, decided to protect a species that was no longer equipped to govern itself.

Bella's story invites us to reflect on what the future might hold: could it be possible that humanity, tired of the conflicts and mistakes of the past, might decide to hand over power to higher intelligences? And if it did, would that be a future of peace and prosperity or a renunciation of everything that makes us human?

9.2 A selfie that no one believes? Critics and theories

Despite the impact Bella's story had on certain online communities, the reception was not entirely positive. In fact, it was her photograph that caused the strongest criticism. The image Bella presented as proof of her visit to the year 3800 quickly became the centre of heated debate. Some were quick to point out what they saw as clear signs of digital manipulation. The shadows, angles and poor quality of the photo led many users to conclude that it was simply a bad edit, a ploy to get attention and viralize her story.

Inconsistencies in the narrative

Critics found several inconsistencies in Bella's narrative that called into question the authenticity of her experience. While Bella described a future in which technologies were so advanced that time travel was possible, many questioned why the quality of the image was so poor if it came from a technologically superior future. Why did a selfie from the year 3800 appear to be of lower quality than photos taken with a smartphone today? These doubts led some to suggest that the photograph was not only manipulated, but was an artistic representation created to provoke controversy and attract a following.

Others pointed to the lack of additional evidence: why didn't she bring with her more objects from the future, something that could corroborate her story beyond a blurred image? The common argument was that, if Bella really had travelled to the year 3800, she should have been able to offer more concrete evidence: records, videos, or even technological artefacts that did not exist in the present.

The Online Debate: Art or Strategy?

On forums and social media, several alternative theories emerged about Bella's true intentions. One popular theory suggested that her story and the photograph were part of an elaborate viral marketing campaign, designed to draw attention to a larger project, such as a science fiction film or even a video game. This theory was fuelled by the increasing use of advertising strategies that masqueraded as viral phenomena, making the public believe they were witnessing something real.

Another theory proposed that Bella might be an artist, and that her whole story was actually an artistic intervention aimed at exploring the fine line between reality and fiction in the digital age. Such projects are not unusual in contemporary art, where the works do not necessarily have to be tangible, but can be collective experiences that challenge the public's perception of what is real and what is invented. Some proponents of this theory argued that Bella was using technology and digital platforms to raise philosophical questions about the impact of technological advances on the way we perceive the world.

The Conspiracy Theory: A Secret Project?

There was, of course, no shortage of conspiracy theories. One of the most widespread suggested that Bella was not simply a time traveller, but part of a much larger, perhaps governmental, project to test how the public would react to the revelation of a robot-controlled future. This theory gained traction when Bella disappeared from the forums where she originally shared her story, leading many to speculate that she had been silenced.

According to this hypothesis, the blurred photo she presented was not a failed test, but an intentional piece of disinformation designed to generate curiosity and get people discussing the possibility of a future governed by artificial intelligences. In this context, Bella would be a covert agent or someone who had been chosen to drop little hints to the public about technologies that are not yet ready to be released. The lack of clarity in her account and her sudden disappearance only further fuelled this conspiratorial narrative.

Bella's Advocates: The Justification for Temporal Distortion

Despite the criticism, a small group of Bella's supporters continued to believe her story. These supporters argued that the technology of time travel, as Bella had described it, had certain limitations that explained the distortion of the photograph. According to them, the very nature of time travel could affect the quality of the physical evidence brought back. This reasoning argued that it was not simply a technical problem, but the extreme and complex conditions involved in time jumping.

These advocates argued that electromagnetic interference, collapsing time fields and other unstable variables during time travel could affect the way the electronics worked, which would explain the poor quality of the image. Furthermore, they claimed that if Bella was lying, she would have presented a much clearer and more convincing picture. The imperfection of the photo was seen by this group as an indication of authenticity, as no one attempting to deceive the public would do so with such weak evidence.

This small but fervent group also argued that, if Bella had been part of a secret experiment, she may not have been allowed to bring more conclusive evidence with her. Limitations imposed by the authorities controlling the experiment would have restricted what she could show publicly, explaining why there were no further objects or records of her experience.

Bella's Silence: A Disturbing Disappearance

Adding even more mystery to the story was Bella's sudden disappearance from social media and forums where she shared her story. After a period of intense activity, where she answered questions and defended her story, Bella stopped posting without warning. This silence generated a flurry of theories and speculation, from those who thought she had been exposed as a fake and decided to withdraw, to those who suggested that she had been forced into silence by the very authorities who were supposedly behind the experiment.

The more conspiratorial fans even raised the possibility that Bella had returned to the future or had been "erased" by powerful entities who did not want the truth to come out. In any case, her disappearance only added fuel to the fire of a story that was already full of unknowns.

Reflections on the controversy

The story of Bella and her famous photograph remains an enigma. For some, it was a clever hoax, a work of fiction designed to attract attention. For others, it was a genuine revelation of a disturbing future, where robots rule the world and humans have been relegated to the background. What is certain is that its story, for all its imperfections, continues to pique the interest and curiosity of those seeking answers about the fate of humanity and the role technology will play in it.

9.3 The rise of viral stories about the future

Bella's story emerged at a crucial moment, when the internet had already become a perfect breeding ground for fantastical tales, conspiracy theories and extraordinary claims to spread at great speed. In that environment, stories like Bella's found an audience hungry for mysteries, uncertain futures, and above all, willing to believe in the unusual, especially if the elements of the narrative touched on collective anxieties and hopes.

The Power of Virality in the Digital Age

In the past, stories about time travellers or supernatural phenomena were transmitted through rumours, science fiction books or traditional media. However, with the advent of social media, the way we interact with such stories has changed dramatically. Platforms such as Twitter, Reddit, YouTube and specialised forums provided an arena where stories could grow exponentially, without any filter or editorial mediation.

Bella's case is a perfect example of how virality works in this context. Despite the fact that she had no conclusive evidence and her photograph was ambiguous at best, her story was shared massively. But what is it that makes such a story gain so much traction? This is where what some experts call "the power of mystery" comes into play. On the internet, a story doesn't need to be verifiable to capture the imagination of thousands of people. Instead, it just needs to arouse curiosity, touch on a relevant social or technological issue, and above all, be easy to share.

Bella's story captured the public's attention not only because of the supposed snapshot of the future, but because it fed into a number of contemporary fears and hopes. In a world increasingly dominated by artificial intelligences, the possibility that robots could replace us was an idea that was already present in the collective mind. Bella arrived at the right time for her story to merge with these pre-existing concerns, turning her story into something bigger than she probably imagined.

Science Fiction and the Influence of Viral Narratives

We cannot ignore the role that science fiction plays in the proliferation of these stories. Since the mid-20th century, we have been exposed to stories exploring time travel, dystopian futures and the rise of artificial intelligences. Series like BLACK MIRROR, films like the MATRIX, or even the TERMINATOR, have shaped our perceptions of the future, preparing us to accept, or at least consider, the possibility that stories like Bella's might have a grain of truth to them.

What is interesting in the case of Bella, and others like it, is how science fiction is intertwined with digital reality. Stories about the future are not only passively consumed through books or films; they are now broadcast and discussed in real time on platforms that allow millions of people to participate. This constant, live interaction between the fictional and the real creates a kind of 'grey zone' where the line between what is possible and what is pure fantasy becomes much more blurred.

Moreover, these viral stories often adapt their narratives in response to public reactions. As Bella's story spread across the web, followers and detractors alike added layers of interpretation, creating new versions and theories. In this way, a story that may initially have been simple begins to branch out and take on different meanings depending on the context in which it is discussed.

The Role of Influencers and Content Creators in Viralization

Another important factor in the rise of viral stories about the future is the role of content creators and influencers. Today, there are thousands of YouTube channels, podcasts and social media accounts dedicated exclusively to analysing and spreading conspiracy theories, mysteries and stories about the future. In Bella's case, her story was quickly picked up by several of these influencers, who made it the subject of their videos and analysis.

What is interesting about this process is that these content creators not only spread the stories, but also reinterpret and reframe them. In Bella's case, some youtubers speculated on the veracity of her selfie, while others connected it to bigger theories, such as the possibility that governments are hiding time travel technologies or that there are "undercover agents" working on secret temporal programmes. Such speculation only served to fuel the virality of the story, making its impact even greater.

The Thirst for Mystery in Modern Society

Another key factor in the rise of viral stories about the future is the public's unquenchable thirst for mystery. In an age where all information seems to be at our fingertips, stories that defy logic and escape immediate explanation are incredibly appealing. Bella's story benefited from this phenomenon. Despite doubts and criticism, the possibility that her story was true continued to resonate in the minds of many people, and that was enough to keep it circulating.

In this sense, viral stories like Bella's do not necessarily depend on authenticity to be popular. What matters is that they feed a curiosity that can never be satiated. In a hyper-connected world, where information flows so fast that it often feels overwhelming, narratives about the future, time travellers or artificial intelligences offer a kind of escape, a portal to a place where the impossible becomes plausible.

The Thin Line between Fact and Fiction

One of the most fascinating elements of the rise of these viral stories is how they alter our perception of reality. When we consume information through the internet, the line between what is real and what is not becomes incredibly thin. Stories about time travellers, such as Bella's, sit right on that border, where fiction can seem more truthful simply because it is easily propagated and constantly repeated.

Forums, social media and video platforms allow these stories to mingle with our everyday concerns about the future. What if Bella really did travel to the year 3800? What if we were about to be replaced by artificial intelligences? These questions are not just exercises in imagination, but are deeply rooted in the real technological advances we experience every day. And it is precisely this mix of fiction and reality that makes stories like Bella's so resonant in contemporary digital culture.

Final Reflection

In short, the story of Bella, the woman who travelled to the year 3800, not only offers a glimpse into a hypothetical future ruled by robots, but also reflects the power of virality in the digital age. What began as a simple forum post ended up capturing the imagination of thousands of people, in large part because of how the narrative fit with the fears and expectations of our society today. Like other stories about time travellers, Bella's story challenges our perceptions of the possible, keeping us intrigued by what might be waiting in the shadows of time.

Chapter 10: Other Incredible Stories of Temporary Travellers

The phenomenon of time travellers is one of the great mysteries that has captured people's imagination over the centuries. The idea of being able to jump between eras, either into the past or the future, has been the subject of countless works of science fiction, conspiracy theories and, for some, even actual experiences. Since the concept of time travel was popularised by literary works such as H.G. Wells' THE TIME MACHINE, the subject has evolved into a fertile ground where reality and fantasy mingle, generating questions that challenge our understanding of time, physics and history.

While a few names, such as John Titor or Bella, have managed to stand out in the modern era, there is a vast ocean of lesser-known but equally astonishing tales. These stories, while often lacking tangible evidence, have not disappeared over time. Indeed, in some cases, they have grown and evolved, fuelled by collective imagination, rumour and speculation. It is in this space where the impossible becomes plausible, and where philosophical questions about fate, causality and the very nature of reality become deeper and more complex.

The Enigma of Time

One of the things that makes time-traveller stories so appealing is that they strike deep chords in our psyche. Who hasn't at some point wished to travel back in time to right a wrong or jump into the future to see what fate has in store for us? These stories invite us to reflect on the power we could have if we had control over time, one of the few constants in our lives that seems inevitable and immutable.

Most people accept that time flows in one direction: forward. However, many accounts of time travellers suggest otherwise. For these so-called travellers, time is malleable, a resource that can be manipulated, broken and twisted. Some modern theories of physics, such as relativity and quantum mechanics, even suggest that time travel may not be completely impossible, at least in theory. This has only added to the fascination with stories claiming that some have broken the barriers of time, albeit without conclusive proof.

Between Science and Fiction

The curious thing about time-traveller stories is that they often inhabit a grey area between science and fiction. While current science tells us that time travel is, at best, extremely difficult, it does not completely rule it out. This small margin of doubt has allowed stories about time travellers to live on in popular culture.

For example, there are theories about wormholes and folds in space-time that could allow time travel. Although these ideas are in the realm of scientific speculation, they fuel the imagination of those who believe that time travel is an undiscovered possibility. Stories of time travellers often rely on these ideas on the fringes of science to give a basis of plausibility to their accounts.

The "Lone Traveller" Narrative

A common pattern in many of these stories is the figure of the "lone traveller". This individual, often a stranger who suddenly appears in the wrong place at the wrong time, brings with him or her tales of distant times, whether from the past or the future. In some cases, these travellers claim to have been sent on specific missions to observe and not intervene, while in others, they claim to have been accidentally caught in a time that does not belong to them.

This type of story captivates us not only because of the possibility of time travel, but also because of what it tells us about our relationship to history and the future. Time travellers often describe dystopian or utopian futures, leading us to wonder about the fate of humanity. These stories act as warnings or promises, inviting us to reflect on the choices we make in the present and their impact on time.

The Element of Intrigue: The Lack of Evidence

Part of the mystery surrounding time travellers lies in the lack of hard evidence. Unlike other paranormal stories or conspiracy theories, accounts of time travel are rarely accompanied by tangible evidence. Instead, they rely on oral testimonies, old letters or blurred photographs that generate more questions than answers.

But this lack of evidence has not caused the stories to lose credibility among those who are willing to believe. In fact, it arguably adds an extra level of intrigue. If these people really had travelled back in time, how could they come back with anything that was irrefutable proof? Is it possible that the technological barriers of time travel could cause physical evidence to deteriorate or be lost in the process? These gaps in evidence open the door to countless theories, each more fascinating than the last.

Legends that Last

If there is one thing these stories of time travellers have in common, it is that, once they emerge, they rarely disappear. Although many of these tales lack solid documentation or have been disproved over time, they continue to circulate in popular culture. Urban legends about time travellers, many of which have been passed on by word of mouth or gone viral on internet forums, continue to fuel the collective imagination. These stories often find a place in the lore of the unexplained, alongside other mysteries such as UFO sightings or paranormal experiences.

Social media has been a key factor in the perpetuation of these legends. Platforms such as YouTube, Reddit and Facebook discussion groups have allowed these stories to be shared and reinterpreted over and over again. For some, these platforms act as digital archives where these stories are collected and analysed, while for others, they become places to generate new versions and theories.

What Makes These Stories So Compelling?

Why are we so fascinated by stories of time travellers? In part, the answer lies in our deep curiosity about the future and the past. These stories offer us a window, however speculative, into what might have been or what might become. Moreover, the idea of being able to change events, alter the course of history or see what the world will be like hundreds of years from now strikes an emotional chord in all of us.

On the other hand, time travel also represents a kind of escape. In a world where many things seem beyond our control, the notion of being able to influence time offers us a sense of power, however fictitious. These stories allow us to dream of the impossible and, at the same time, to question what we take for granted about reality.

10.1 Who are the other lesser-known travellers?

The phenomenon of time travel is full of fascinating characters, many of whom have remained in the shadows of mystery. These tales, while not as celebrated as those of more well-known figures, have captured the imagination of those who believe that time is malleable and that it is possible to move through it. Below, we explore some of the lesser-known but equally intriguing characters.

1. Paul Amadeus Dienach: The Man Who Woke Up in the Future

The story of Paul Amadeus Dienach is one of the most intriguing in the world of time travel, not because it involves advanced technology or time machines, but because of its purely mental or spiritual nature. In 1921, Dienach, a 36-year-old Swiss professor, fell into a coma due to complications related to tuberculosis. What followed was a full year of unconsciousness - or so it seemed from the outside.

During that year, Dienach claimed that his consciousness was transported to the year **3906**, a time when humanity was nothing like what we know today. According to his account, while his body was in a coma in 1921, his mind inhabited the body of a man named **Andreas Northam**, an important figure in this distant future. What Dienach experienced and saw during that time is the central theme of his work **The Chronicles of the Future**, a manuscript that many consider prophetic, though it remains shrouded in mystery.

Humanity in the Year 3906: A Perfect Future or an Illusion?

One of the most fascinating aspects of Dienach's story is his description of humanity in the year 3906. In his words, society had overcome the conflicts that today seem inevitable: there were no wars, no poverty, no gender or racial conflicts. Humanity had reached a level of **spiritual perfection** that we can scarcely imagine today. This leap in human evolution was not based solely on technological advances, but on a profound philosophical and spiritual transformation. The human beings of the future, according to Dienach, lived in harmony not only with each other, but also with the environment and the forces of the universe.

Interestingly, Dienach did not describe a hyper-technological society as science fiction futures are often presented. Although technology existed and was advanced, it did not dominate people's lives. Instead, it was spirituality and connection to the cosmos that defined this era. This detail has intrigued many, as it goes against the typical futuristic narrative where technology overshadows human life.

How did you arrive at this future?

One of the most mysterious points of Dienach's account is the way in which his time "travel" occurred. Unlike conventional accounts of time travellers, there was no time machine, failed experiment or cosmic accident. Instead, his journey was entirely **mental**. While his body lay motionless in a hospital, his consciousness "jumped" into the future and inhabited another body. This leads to some disturbing questions: Is it possible that our minds can transcend time and space? Could time not be linear, but rather a series of states that our consciousnesses can traverse?

Dienach did not consider himself a scientist or a paranormal researcher. In fact, upon returning to his original time and body, he simply tried to process what he had experienced. He decided to write down his story in a detailed manuscript, not with the intention of publishing it, but as a personal way of documenting what he had experienced.

The Chronicles of the Future: An Almost Lost Testimony

Dienach's manuscript, known as **The Chronicles of the Future**, was never published during his lifetime. In fact, Dienach did not seek fame or recognition for his account. When he died in 1924, he gave his manuscript to one of his students, **George Papachatzis**, who was shocked by its contents and kept it secret for many years. It was Papachatzis who later decided to share the document with a small circle of people interested in esotericism and the mysteries of time.

The text details Dienach's experiences in Northam's body and describes a future in which political, economic and social barriers no longer existed. According to the manuscript, humanity had evolved into a near-universal species, connected at a deep level to the energy and secrets of the cosmos. Cities were vast and glittering, but they did not pollute or destroy nature. In fact, the balance between technology and ecology was one of the keys to this new era.

The questions raised by Dienach: Is this possible?

Dienach's story raises many questions, but one of the most intriguing is: **Is it possible that our minds can travel through time, even if our bodies cannot?** This idea has been explored in science and philosophy for years, but has never been taken completely seriously. However, accounts such as Dienach's suggest that there may be more to the nature of consciousness and time than we understand.

Another interesting question is the following: **If Dienach really did experience the year 3906, why has this phenomenon not been repeated -** was it a unique event, or are there other cases like his that have never come to light? With no concrete evidence beyond his written account, these questions remain unanswered, but his story continues to fuel the imagination of those who believe that time is not a rigid line, but a vast field of possibilities.

A future few believe in

Despite his fascinating account, Dienach's story has been met with scepticism, even within esoteric circles. The lack of tangible evidence and the unusual nature of his 'journey' lead many to see it as a mere fantasy or the result of an altered mental state due to his illness. However, for those who study the nature of time and consciousness, his testimony remains one of the most interesting, precisely because it deviates from the typical conventions of time travel.

The fact that **The Chronicles of the Future** was never formally published during Dienach's lifetime adds an air of mystery. Why would someone who claims to have seen the fate of humanity not seek to make this information public? The answer, some say, may lie in the fear of being ridiculed or not being taken seriously. Others, however, suggest that Dienach believed that the world was not ready to receive the message he had brought from the future.

2. Sir Victor Goddard: The temporary slip of an RAF Officer

In 1935, **Sir Victor Goddard**, a respected British Royal Air Force (RAF) officer, had a perplexing experience that remains to this day one of the most puzzling cases of possible "time slips". While flying over an abandoned airfield in **Drem**, Scotland, in the middle of a severe storm, Goddard witnessed an unexplained phenomenon. What began as a simple reconnaissance mission turned out to be one of the most intriguing accounts of possible time travel.

The Storm That Unleashed the Mystery

Sir Victor Goddard had been sent on a routine mission to inspect various airfields and their state of repair. One of the sites he was to observe was **Drem** airfield in Scotland, which at the time was in a state of complete disrepair. The runway was in disrepair, overgrown with vegetation, and the buildings around it were crumbling. However, on his return flight, he encountered an unusually violent storm. Wind and rain lashed his plane, hampering visibility and forcing him to fly through the storm.

Suddenly, and without warning, the storm stopped, as if a curtain had been lifted. The sky, previously obscured by clouds and rain, cleared abruptly and strangely. What Goddard saw next was completely disconcerting: **the Drem airfield** no longer appeared to be abandoned.

Instead, what he saw was a fully restored and fully operational airfield. Aircraft were lined up on the runway, and personnel were working diligently, as if everything was up and running at an active air base.

What Goddard Observed in Drem

What was most intriguing about Goddard's vision was not only the fact that the Drem airfield, which minutes before had been in ruins, appeared to be in perfect condition. There was something even stranger: **the aircraft and personnel did not match what he had known at the time**. The aircraft he saw were of a different type, painted a yellow colour that was not common in the RAF at the time. In addition, the mechanics and ground crew wore blue uniforms, which were also not standard at the time.

At the time, Goddard could not comprehend what he was seeing. To him, it seemed as if he had been transported, for a brief moment, to a future that did not yet exist. After flying over the airfield for a few more minutes, the storm reappeared as quickly as it had disappeared, and Goddard again found himself battling the bad weather to return to his base. Although he was sure of what he had seen, he could not explain it, and decided to keep the experience to himself for a while.

Airfield Restoration: The Future Goddard Witnessed

Years later, in 1939, **World War II** broke out, and the Drem airfield was renovated for use by the RAF. What puzzled Sir Victor Goddard was that the renovation of the airfield matched **exactly** what he had seen on his 1935 flight. The RAF training aircraft had been repainted yellow, just like the ones he had seen during his flight, and the ground crew had begun wearing blue uniforms. The airfield had been completely refurbished and modernised, matching the vision Goddard had had during that strange experience in the storm.

It is this detail that makes Goddard's account one of the most intriguing accounts of time slippage. Not only did he see something unexplainable at the time, but events years later seem to confirm that what he saw was a **glimpse into the future**. Rather than being a simple hallucination or misunderstanding, the restoration of the airfield suggests that, for some unknown reason, Goddard had witnessed what would happen years later.

How to Explain Goddard's Time Slip?

Sir Victor Goddard's experience remains an enigma. Although many theories have been proposed, none can fully explain what happened.

Some theories suggest that Goddard may have experienced a **time slip** phenomenon, an anomaly in which time momentarily folds and allows a person to observe events that have not yet occurred or have already occurred.

Another possibility is that the intense storm somehow affected Goddard's perception, although this explanation seems less likely, given that what he saw eventually materialised in reality years later. It has also been speculated that the time slips could be related to **fluctuations in space-time**, a concept that quantum physics is just beginning to explore. According to this theory, certain climatic or electromagnetic events could cause ruptures in the space-time continuum, allowing people to briefly see or experience other times.

Although Goddard never claimed to have understood what happened to him, he was convinced that what he saw was real. And the coincidence between his vision and the subsequent restoration of the airfield only added credibility to his account.

Accidental Time Travel?

Sir Victor Goddard's story raises the fascinating possibility that **time travel**, in certain circumstances, could occur without direct human intervention. In this case, there were no time machines or advanced technology; it was simply an RAF officer on a routine mission. While accounts of time slippage are not as common as other types of paranormal experiences, what makes them fascinating is that they are often unintentional and disconcerting to those who experience them.

Goddard's story has become a classic case for those who study the mysteries of time. The fact that a respected military officer with a long career reported such a bizarre event adds a level of seriousness that many other cases lack. Moreover, it is the fact that his vision was accurately fulfilled years later that makes this case one of the most compelling on the possibility that time is not an immutable constant.

Final Reflections: Drem's Slide

The case of Sir Victor Goddard continues to fascinate those interested in time travel and unexplained phenomena. Although almost 90 years have passed since Goddard had his experience at Drem Airfield, his account remains one of the most intriguing examples of temporal slippage. The idea that a storm could open a window into the future raises questions about the very nature of time and reality.

Is it possible that there are **moments or places** where time slips unpredictably, allowing us to glimpse the future or the past? Or was Goddard's experience simply an extraordinary coincidence? While we cannot answer these questions with certainty, his account reminds us that there is still much we do not know about the workings of time and the universe.

3. Jophar Vorin: Man from an unknown land

The story of **Jophar Vorin** is one of those that, despite being less well known, continues to generate unanswered questions. In 1851, this mysterious man appeared in a small town in **Frankfurt an der Oder**, Germany, claiming to be from a place called **Laxaria**, a country he said was located in a region of the world known as **Sakria**. The puzzling thing about the case is that neither Laxaria nor Sakria appear on any map, nor did they then, nor do they today. But what makes this story so intriguing is not only the lack of geographical evidence for the existence of these places, but the details of their history and the inexplicable nature of their origin.

The Apparition of Jophar Vorin: A Baffling Mystery

The man, who called himself **Jophar Vorin**, was discovered in a state of confusion and disorientation by local authorities. He was dressed strangely, in clothes that did not quite conform to the styles of the time in Germany. He spoke a completely unknown language, but through a mixture of **European languages**, mainly German and Latin, he managed to make himself understood. He explained to the authorities that he came from **Laxaria**, a country in a vast region of the world called **Sakria**, and that he was looking for his brothers, who had disappeared at sea.

What puzzled the authorities was that, despite attempts to locate his country of origin, **Laxaria was not on any map** and no one had ever heard of Sakria. Vorin's story became stranger and stranger as the details emerged: how had a man from a non-existent country come to this small German town? And how could he possibly speak familiar languages but come from a completely unknown culture?

Unknown Language and Communication

Although Jophar Vorin did not speak any known language in its entirety, he was able to communicate partially through a mixture of several European languages, mostly a variant of Latin. Scholars at the time were puzzled by this fact, as it seemed that Vorin came from a civilisation that shared roots with Latin, but had evolved completely independently.

Some even speculated that this language might have been a remnant of a **lost civilisation** or a remnant of a parallel world, leading to theories about the existence of **alternate dimensions**. Could it be that Jophar Vorin came from a **parallel reality** in which Laxaria was an existing country, but which in our world is simply not recorded? While this sounds unbelievable, it is one of the few theories that have been proposed to explain his origin.

A Time Traveller or an Inhabitant of a Parallel Dimension?

The more outlandish theories suggest that Jophar Vorin may have been a **time traveller**, someone who had somehow been transported from a completely different time or reality to our own. At the time, the idea of time travel was not as much a part of the popular imagination as it is today, but many believe that stories like Vorin's could be early examples of people who accidentally became trapped in **a different timeline**.

Another hypothesis that has gained momentum over the years is the idea that Jophar Vorin may have come from an **alternate dimension**. According to this theory, a phenomenon could have occurred in which the borders between dimensions were temporarily blurred, allowing Vorin to cross into our reality without being aware of it. This would explain why he came from a country that did not exist on our maps, but perhaps did exist in his own reality.

The Disappearance of Jophar Vorin: The End of the Mystery

What makes Jophar Vorin's account even more puzzling is the fact that, after being examined by the authorities and the brightest minds of the time, **he disappeared without a trace**. It is not known what happened to him after his case was registered, and no further details of his whereabouts were found. Some accounts say he was taken to Berlin for further questioning, but there is no record of what happened after that.

His disappearance adds an additional layer of mystery to his story: was he taken to some secret location to be investigated by the government of the time, or did he somehow simply return to the dimension or time he came from? In the absence of conclusive evidence, the story of Jophar Vorin has remained one of those unexplained cases that defy our understanding of reality.

Modern Theories

Over time, the case of Jophar Vorin has been revisited by paranormal enthusiasts, who have offered various explanations. Some suggest that he may have been a **fugitive** who concocted a fantastic story to avoid capture, or that perhaps he was suffering from a mental disorder that led him to believe his account. Others, however, are adamant that Jophar Vorin may have been proof of the existence of **parallel universes** or **time travel**.

In recent years, the story has been discussed in conspiracy theories and esoteric forums, with some even suggesting that his case was covered up by the authorities to avoid panic or speculation. While there is no concrete evidence that this is true, what is certain is that the story of Jophar Vorin has managed to persist in the collective memory as one of the most puzzling accounts of people who seem to have come from places that should not exist.

Final Reflections

The case of Jophar Vorin remains a mystery that defies logic. The lack of conclusive evidence and the man's sudden disappearance only add to the enigma: was Jophar Vorin a **time traveller**, an inhabitant of a **parallel dimension**, or simply someone with an elaborate history? Although it is impossible to reach a definitive conclusion, his story continues to fascinate those seeking answers about what is beyond our understanding.

Jophar Vorin's story reminds us that there are many mysteries in the world, some of which simply cannot be explained by conventional logic. What if there are other realities, other times or places that co-exist with our own but remain beyond our reach? Whatever the truth behind Jophar Vorin's story, it remains a warning that the world is far more vast and complex than we often imagine.

4. The Cape Scott Traveller

Canada's **Cape Scott** coast is known for its wild beauty, but also for its isolation. This place, famous among hikers and adventurers, became the setting for one of the most puzzling accounts of possible time travellers. In **1973**, a group of hikers touring the area reported an encounter with a mysterious man who seemed disoriented and out of place, as if he belonged to another time.

The Encounter with the Disoriented Man

According to the hikers' account, while walking along one of **Cape Scott'**s trails, they came across a man wandering aimlessly. The first thing that struck them was his appearance: he was wearing clothes that did not correspond to the fashion of the 1970s. He wore a long coat, in the style of the early 20th century, and his shoes, worn and old, were unsuitable for the rocky terrain of the area. He also looked **confused and frightened**, as if he did not understand where he was or how he had gotten there.

The hikers tried to talk to him, but he did not respond coherently. His attitude was strange, and he seemed unaware of his surroundings. As they approached, the man seemed to panic and, without warning, **mysteriously disappeared** before their eyes. The strangest thing was that, at the spot where he had been, they found an **old camera**. This object would be the only physical evidence left of the encounter.

The Photographic Camera: Key to the Mystery

The camera that the mysterious man left behind was, according to experts, an old model, which had not been used since the early 20th century. Intriguingly, the camera still had a roll of film inside, prompting the hikers to hand it over to the authorities to be developed. The images they found on the film only added to the mystery of the case.

The photos showed people dressed in **old** clothes, clearly from a time before the 1970s. Some images appeared to be of landscapes, but none matched the known areas of **Cape Scott** or the surrounding area. The people in the photos also could not be identified. There were no signs connecting this man to any local community or other known historical records, leading to speculation that the man was a **time traveller** trapped outside his own time.

Theories about the Cape Scott Traveller

The Cape Scott event has given rise to numerous theories, many of them centred on the idea that the man could have been an accidental **time traveller**. One of the most popular explanations is that he could have been a person from the early 20th century who was somehow transported to the future, specifically 1973, without understanding what had happened.

Theories about **temporal anomalies** in certain places are not new. Some researchers suggest that in remote, naturally energetic places, such as

Cape Scott, phenomena that affect time and space could occur. These "anomalies" could cause people to be transported briefly between different epochs, with no control over the situation. The man the hikers encountered may have fallen victim to one of these temporal anomalies, becoming trapped in a time and place he did not recognise.

Another theory suggests that the man may have been **moving between different dimensions** or parallel realities. This would explain why his clothes and camera were from another era, but not necessarily from our own historical past. According to this theory, the man could have come from a slightly different reality to ours, where fashions and technology were similar but not identical. His sudden disappearance could have been the result of his "return" to that alternate dimension.

The Unexplained Disappearance

The most puzzling part of the story is the disappearance of the man. The hikers saw him vanish before their eyes without a trace, except for the camera. The authorities investigated the case, but found no further evidence that could explain what happened. There was no evidence that the man was a local resident or a visitor from a nearby town. His identity remains a complete mystery, and no one has been able to offer a plausible explanation for his sudden appearance and disappearance.

Although many theories have been proposed, none have been able to conclusively explain what happened at Cape Scott in 1973. The lack of additional information and the man's disappearance without trace have left this case in the realm of the unexplained.

The Camera: Last Piece of the Puzzle

The camera remains the only physical piece of evidence linking this incident to reality. The images, though mostly incomprehensible, remain the most tangible proof that something strange happened that day. Some have suggested that there may be more information hidden in these images, but with the technology of the time, it was not possible to obtain more precise details. As the film degraded over time, the hope of discovering more about the man's identity faded.

To this day, the incident at Cape Scott remains an unsolved mystery. For the more sceptical, it could be a simple case of confusion or a mentally disturbed person seen by the hikers. However, for those who believe in the possibility of time travel or dimensional anomalies, this is a classic case of a traveller trapped in the wrong time.

Final Reflections: Accidental Time Travel

The story of the Cape Scott traveller leaves us with more questions than answers. Who was this man? Where did he come from and how did he end up in that place, at that time? Is it possible that Cape Scott is one of those places where temporal anomalies occur, allowing people from different eras to slip between time and space?

What makes this case particularly disturbing is the lack of a logical explanation. The disappearance of the man, the ancient camera and the photos that could not be identified add layers of mystery that have never been solved. Whatever the truth, the Cape Scott traveller remains one of the most puzzling accounts of possible **time travel**, fuelling speculation and fascination with the unexplained.

5. Charlotte Anne Moberly and Eleanor Jourdain: The Incident at Versailles

One of the most puzzling accounts of time slippage is that of British academics **Charlotte Anne Moberly** and **Eleanor Jourdain**, who in **1901** claimed to have experienced what they described as a "journey into the past" while visiting the famous **Palace of Versailles** in France. Although many have tried to discredit their story, their experience remains one of the most documented and debated cases of possible time travel. What Moberly and Jourdain experienced was not only a visual experience, but both claimed to have witnessed a historical scene that should not have existed.

The Visit to Versailles

On 10 August 1901, Charlotte Anne Moberly, Provost of **St Hugh's College, Oxford,** and her colleague **Eleanor Jourdain** visited the Palace of Versailles as part of a trip to France. Both scholars were educated women, accustomed to critical and scientific analysis, which makes their account all the more intriguing. Their aim was to see the gardens and explore the history of the French monarchy, especially the period of Marie Antoinette. However, what they experienced was something they could not have anticipated.

While walking through the vast gardens of Versailles, the two women said they felt a change in the atmosphere. They described how everything suddenly **seemed heavier and stranger**, as if an invisible fog had enveloped the place. The atmosphere was oppressive, and both began to feel disconcerted. It was at this point that they began to see people who did not seem to belong to their time.

Visions of the Past

According to their account, Moberly and Jourdain saw several people **dressed in 18th century style**, including a man in a wig and a woman dressed in Marie Antoinette-era clothing. As they walked along, both described sensing that **something was not right**. The music playing in the background and the very sounds of the surroundings did not correspond to the Versailles they knew in the present. It was as if they had been transported to a completely different era.

The most extraordinary thing was that, according to Moberly, they both came across a woman sitting on the lawn, quietly sketching. Moberly was convinced that this woman was none other than **Marie Antoinette** herself, the famous queen of France. The woman they saw had a sharp face and elegant attire, features that matched the portraits of the queen. Although they did not interact directly with these figures, they both felt they were out of time, as if they had witnessed a scene that belonged to the past.

Confusion and the Return to Reality

After this strange encounter, the two women continued to walk through the gardens, but noticed that the surreal atmosphere was gradually fading. Soon they found themselves back among contemporary tourists and the usual hustle and bustle of Versailles. However, neither of them could ignore what had just happened. Both felt they had witnessed something beyond rational comprehension.

Upon returning to England, Moberly and Jourdain discussed their experience and decided to write down their observations separately. What they found was surprising: their accounts coincided in many details, which reinforced their belief that they had indeed experienced something extraordinary. The descriptions they gave of the gardens and the people they saw corresponded to **18th century Versailles**, although some of the details were no longer visible in the present, such as certain buildings or paths that no longer existed.

The Book: "AN ADVENTURE"

Convinced of the authenticity of their experience, in 1911, Moberly and Jourdain published a book under pseudonyms entitled "AN ADVENTURE" detailing their encounter at Versailles and the people they saw. In the book, they described what they believed to be a temporal slip, a phenomenon in which they were somehow transported back in time for a brief moment.

The book immediately generated controversy. While some readers were fascinated by the story, others dismissed it as a shared hallucination or even a fantasy invented by the authors. However, Moberly and Jourdain insisted to the end of their lives that what they experienced was real and not a figment of their imagination. The two women, who were respected academics, never gave any indication that they had invented the story for sensationalist purposes.

Theories and Explanations

Over the years, multiple explanations have been offered for the bizarre incident at Versailles. Some have suggested that Moberly and Jourdain may have been under the effects of a **shared hallucination**, a rare but documented condition in which two people simultaneously experience an altered perception of reality. However, the detailed nature of their accounts, as well as their ability to accurately describe certain aspects of Versailles that no longer existed in 1901, has led many to dismiss this explanation.

Another theory that has gained traction is the possibility that Moberly and Jourdain may have experienced a phenomenon known as **residual memory** or **psychic imprinting**. According to this theory, certain places steeped in history, such as the Palace of Versailles, may 'imprint' moments from the past on their surroundings. Under certain conditions, these impressions can manifest themselves again, allowing people to see scenes from the past as if they were happening in the present.

Finally, the most intriguing explanation is that both women experienced a genuine **time slip**, a phenomenon in which for some unknown reason, time folded momentarily, allowing them to witness events that occurred centuries earlier. This theory, though difficult to prove, is one that has captured the imagination of time-travel enthusiasts, as it suggests that time may not be an immutable constant.

The Legacy of the Incident at Versailles

Although Moberly and Jourdain's story has been the subject of scepticism, it remains one of the most famous accounts of possible time travel. The idea that two highly educated and respected women in academia could have invented or misinterpreted an experience of this magnitude seems improbable to many. Moreover, the fact that their accounts coincided so closely, and that the descriptions they gave corresponded to historical details of Versailles that no longer existed, makes their story still intriguing.

Today, the case of the "Versailles incident" continues to be studied by those interested in paranormal phenomena and time slippage. The possibility that time can be malleable, and that places steeped in history can "relive" their past, raises fascinating questions about the nature of time and our ability to perceive it.

Final Reflections

The case of **Charlotte Anne Moberly** and **Eleanor Jourdain** is a reminder that even in modern times, the inexplicable can appear in the most unexpected places. While the Palace of Versailles is a symbol of power and opulence, it has also become a place where the impossible seems to have happened. Was the Moberly and Jourdain incident a genuine journey into the past or simply an illusion? The fact that the two academics, both rational and prestigious people, defended their account to the end suggests that what they experienced in 1901 was much more than just a fantasy.

6. Noah Novak: The 2030 Traveller

In recent years, the appearance of people who claim to be **time travellers** has found fertile ground on social networks to go viral. Among them, one of the most notorious cases is that of **Noah Novak**, who appeared on various digital platforms around **2018**, claiming to be from the year **2030**. Unlike other accounts of time travel that focus on much more distant times, Novak claimed to come from a relatively near future, where humanity had experienced significant advances in technology, but also faced significant challenges.

Novak's Predictions: A Future Controlled by Artificial Intelligence

Noah Novak describes a future where **artificial intelligence (AI)** and **automation** have reached such a level of development that much of human activity is controlled by autonomous systems. According to Novak, in his time, most physical and administrative jobs had been completely replaced by **machines** and **algorithms**, with both benefits and negative consequences. Although everyday life was made more comfortable by automation, there was also growing **social discontent** due to mass unemployment and loss of autonomy in decision-making.

One of the most worrying aspects of the future he described was the growing influence of **centralised artificial intelligence**, which controlled not only infrastructure and financial systems, but also many political decisions. According to Novak, governments of the future had delegated a considerable amount of power to these AIs, generating great controversy among those who feared they would lose control over their lives completely.

The Details of Your Story: A World of Progress and Conflict

In his numerous video appearances and interviews, Novak provided specific details about what life would be like in **2030**. According to him, technology had advanced so far that current devices, such as smartphones and computers, had been replaced by **neural interfaces** that allowed humans to connect directly to the network with their thoughts. This advance had completely transformed the way people interacted with the digital world and with other people.

In addition, Novak said that **climate change** had worsened dramatically in the years leading up to 2030, causing large migrations and conflicts in different regions of the world. Coastal cities were at risk from rising sea levels, and many of the world's most powerful economies were struggling to adapt to this new reality. However, according to Novak, technological advances in renewable energy had enabled humanity to avoid a global catastrophe.

On the other hand, he described a deeply divided world: while some countries had embraced **full automation**, others still struggled with obsolete technologies and economic problems. This division had led to a series of global conflicts between technologically advanced nations and those that had been left behind. The struggle for resources and access to technology was a major cause of tension in this near future.

Society's Disenchantment with AI

One of the most interesting points in Noah Novak's account is the **disenchantment** that society in 2030 felt towards AI. According to Novak, while automation had initially been greeted with optimism, the increasing control that AIs exerted over human decisions had begun to generate resistance. Citizens felt increasingly marginalised, powerless over their own lives, as AIs made political, economic and even personal decisions. This loss of control led to a resistance movement known as the **"humanists of the future"**, who fought to regain human autonomy.

Novak described this movement as an ideological struggle in which "humanists" believed that humanity should take a more active role in decision-making, rather than relying entirely on machines. However, in his future, this resistance was in the minority and not very successful, as the majority of the population preferred the convenience that AI offered, even if it meant sacrificing their individual freedom.

Controversy and Criticism

Despite the intriguing nature of his predictions, **Noah Novak** has not been without criticism. Like many other so-called time travellers, the lack of tangible evidence has led many people to accuse him of being a **fraud** or simply seeking notoriety on social media. Several of his key predictions, which were scheduled to come true in 2020, failed to materialise, fuelling scepticism about his story.

Among the most flawed predictions was the claim that by 2020, the world would have begun to massively deploy **fusion energy**, which would solve the problems of energy shortages and reduce dependence on fossil fuels. Although fusion research is still ongoing, we are a long way from having reached mass use of this technology, which casts doubt on the accuracy of his account.

In addition, Novak also predicted that in 2020 there would be a **major economic crisis** caused by the collapse of several central banks due to **cryptocurrency** technology. While the use of cryptocurrencies has grown, there has not been a global collapse of the banking system as he predicted.

Virality in the Modern Age

Despite these inconsistencies, Noah Novak remains a recurring character in **internet forums and social networks** dedicated to time travel theories. The intriguing nature of his account, coupled with a general fascination with technology and artificial intelligence, has kept discussion about its authenticity alive. Some proponents suggest that Novak's predictions were simply temporally misaligned, and that he was actually describing events that could occur later than predicted.

In some circles, Novak is seen as a warning about what could happen if humanity continues to delegate too much power to machines. For others, it is simply another attempt to viralize a story without evidence. However, its ability to capture attention and generate discussion about the future is undeniable.

Final Reflections: A Possible Future or Science Fiction?

Noah Novak's case raises a number of important questions about the future of humanity and the relationship with artificial intelligence. Although many of his predictions have not come true, his account reflects real concerns that are already beginning to emerge today: the growing role of automation in our lives, the impact of climate change and the struggle for control in an increasingly technological world.

Regardless of whether Novak is a genuine time traveller or simply a convincing storyteller, his story serves as a warning about the direction humanity could take. Are we really prepared for a future in which machines make decisions for us? Is artificial intelligence a tool that will liberate humanity or a system that will end up enslaving us? Only time will tell whether Novak's predictions were visionary or simply fantasy.

7. Alexander Smith: The man from 2118

In **2018**, a man calling himself **Alexander Smith** appeared in several YouTube videos and similar platforms claiming to have travelled to the future, specifically to the year **2118**. According to him, his experience was not the result of an accident, but part of a **secret CIA project** designed to explore the future of humanity. Throughout his interviews, Smith described a future filled with **advanced technology**, but also one in which society faced significant challenges under the control of a centralised artificial intelligence. Although Smith presented a blurry photograph as proof of his journey, his story has largely been met with scepticism. Still, it remains a recurring theme in forums and communities exploring conspiracy theories.

The Alexander Smith Story: A Future of Technology and Control

Alexander Smith described a future that, for many, sounds like something out of a science fiction film. In the year **2118**, according to his account, cities were **futuristic megalopolises**, with skyscrapers that seemed to touch the sky and **flying vehicles** that crisscrossed the skies. Transport systems had been completely revolutionised, and interplanetary travel was a common reality for humanity. However, behind this utopian image of technological progress, Smith also painted a future in which humanity was increasingly controlled by **artificial intelligence**.

According to Smith, artificial intelligence not only regulated infrastructure and everyday services, but had assumed a **dominant** role **in political decision-making**. World leaders had become dependent on these AIs for everything from economic planning to social surveillance. Although life in general was more comfortable, many humans lived in a state of **technological subservience**, where important decisions about their lives were made by machines.

In addition, he described a world where **climate change** had worsened severely, forcing much of the world's population to live in **cities under domes** to protect themselves from extreme weather conditions. The oceans had risen significantly, flooding much of the coastal cities, and many regions of the world had become uninhabitable. Resources were managed extremely efficiently, but only with the help of an artificial intelligence that controlled every aspect of life on Earth.

The Photograph of the Future: Proof or Fake?

One of the most intriguing aspects of Alexander Smith's account was the **blurred photograph** he presented as proof of his journey into the future. In the image, one could see what he described as a **futuristic city**, with buildings of unknown architecture and floating vehicles. However, the quality of the photograph was extremely poor, which provoked a wave of scepticism.

Critics were quick to point out that the image could have been digitally manipulated or simply taken from a science fiction film. The lack of clarity and detail in the photograph led many to dismiss his story as an **elaborate hoax**. However, for some of his followers, the photograph was sufficient evidence to back up his account, and many believed that the inconsistencies in quality could have been due to the technological limitations of the alleged equipment with which he took it.

Moreover, Smith insisted that he could not bring back clearer evidence because of the **restrictions imposed by the CIA** and other government agencies that had controlled his trip. According to him, there were strict rules about what information he could share, and his life was in danger for revealing even the most basic details of his experience.

The CIA's Secret Project

One of the most fascinating points in Smith's account is his claim that he had been part of a **secret CIA time travel project**. According to him, this programme was developed over decades and used advanced technology to send people to different points in time, both past and future. Although he did not give many details about how this technology worked, he mentioned that time travel was related to experiments in quantum physics and the use of **electromagnetic energy** to create time tunnels.

Smith claimed that the CIA had been working on this technology since the 1980s and that he had been selected as one of the first time travellers. He claimed that his mission was to gather information about the state of the world in the year 2118 to help current governments prepare for future challenges. While this idea may seem far-fetched, some connect it to broader conspiracy theories about government control and secret experimentation with the physics of time.

Scepticism and Criticism

Despite the intriguing nature of his account, **Alexander Smith** has been the subject of criticism and scepticism since he first appeared in 2018. Like other alleged time travellers, the lack of solid evidence has led many to dismiss him as a fraud. The blurry photograph he submitted was analysed by imaging experts, who suggested it was likely a digital montage or manipulated image.

Furthermore, the idea that the **CIA** is involved in a time travel programme has been dismissed as an unsubstantiated conspiracy theory. Although there are reports that government agencies have experimented with advanced technologies, there is no credible evidence that time travel has been possible.

Another criticism is that Smith has offered no **verifiable predictions** about future events that could support his story. Unlike other alleged time travellers, Smith has not provided specific details about impending events that could be easily confirmed or refuted. This has led many to believe that his account is simply a fabrication, designed to gain notoriety on the internet.

The Impact on Conspiracy Culture

Despite the criticism, Alexander Smith has found an audience willing to listen to his stories. In conspiracy theory forums and time travel communities, his story continues to be discussed, especially by those who believe that governments are withholding information about advanced technologies and secret projects. In these circles, the idea that **artificial intelligence** could control the future is not so far-fetched, and Smith's story resonates as a warning about the dangers of delegating too much power to machines.

For many of his supporters, Alexander Smith's story is a reminder that there are forces at play that the general public is not aware of. They believe that time travel could be a reality, but that governments have kept these advances hidden for reasons of national security. Although his account has not been verified, it remains a symbol of the **distrust** that many feel towards governments and technology corporations in the modern era.

Final Reflections: A Dystopian Future or Science Fiction?

Alexander Smith's story raises disturbing questions about the future of humanity and the role of artificial intelligence. While his account lacks concrete evidence, many of the issues he addresses - such as AI control, climate change and authoritarian governments - are very real concerns that humanity already faces.

While we will probably never know if Alexander Smith actually travelled to the year 2118, his story remains a warning about a possible dystopian future in which machines control our lives and governments use advanced technologies to hide the truth from the public. Is this a glimpse of what might be coming or simply a fictional story designed to capture attention? The truth, as with so many other time travel stories, remains a mystery.

8. The man from Taured

The case of the **Taured man** is one of the most enigmatic examples in the world of unsolved mysteries. In **1954**, a man was arrested at **Haneda airport** in Tokyo, Japan, for what appeared to be an irregularity with his passport. So far, it might seem like just another case of forged documents or a simple bureaucratic misunderstanding. However, what made this incident an inexplicable phenomenon was the fact that the man **claimed to be from a country that did not exist on any map**, a country called **Taured**.

The Arrival of the Mysterious Man

The man, who looked to be in his 40s and 50s, arrived at Haneda airport on an apparently normal day. He was dressed in a typical costume of the time, and spoke several languages fluently, including **French** and **Japanese**. He reportedly carried a perfectly valid passport, issued by the country of **Taured**. The document was full of stamps from previous trips, indicating that he had visited many countries before, and all the stamps appeared to be authentic.

However, when the immigration authorities checked his passport, something didn't add up: **Taured didn't exist**. The officials asked him several times where he was from, and the man insisted that he came from a country called Taured, located between **France and Spain**, in what is now known as **Andorra**. What was puzzling was that the man seemed completely genuine and surprised to discover that Taured did not exist on maps at the time. According to him, his country had existed for centuries.

The Legitimate Documents and the Geographical Mystery

The man was carrying more than just a passport. He was also carrying a **driver's licence** issued in Taured, and business documents showing that he had travelled to Japan on business. The authorities tried to search for any record of his country, but found absolutely nothing. There was no **country called Taured** in the modern world, and the closest thing to the location he described was the Principality of Andorra.

Unable to verify his origin, officials began to suspect that the man might be involved in some kind of **forgery** or crime. Despite this, all his documents appeared legitimate, there was no sign of tampering or forgery. Confusion reigned at the airport, as they could not explain how someone with apparently valid documents from a non-existent country had got there.

The Unexplained Disappearance

Determined to investigate the matter further, the Japanese authorities decided to hold the man in a **nearby hotel** while they continued to investigate his identity. He was placed in custody in a room with guards guarding the door throughout the night. His belongings, including his documents and passport, were held for further investigation by experts.

The next morning, when the officers entered the room to continue the interrogation, **the man had disappeared without a trace**. There was no sign of an escape: the window was not open and the guards did not see anyone enter or leave the room. Quite simply, the man from Taured had inexplicably disappeared, along with all his documents.

It was this abrupt and mysterious end that sealed the case of the Taured man as one of the most puzzling in history. The Japanese authorities investigated the disappearance, but were unable to find any clues as to his whereabouts. It was as if the man had never existed, as if he had been wiped off the face of the earth, along with his fictitious country.

Alternate Realities or Temporary Slips?

The case of the man from Taured has generated a great deal of speculation and theories over the years. One of the most fascinating theories is that the man may have been a **traveller from a parallel reality**, someone who accidentally crossed into our dimension from a world where Taured exists as a legitimate country. According to this theory, there are infinite alternate realities, and in some of them, the geography, history and countries may be different from ours. The man from Taured would have somehow crossed over into our reality, but he still believed he was in his own world.

Another popular theory is that the man was the victim of a **time slip**, in which, through some anomaly, he crossed through time or space from a different time or dimension. These temporal slips suggest that certain places or moments may be connected to specific points in time or other realities, allowing people or things to move between them without realising it. For the man from Taured, it could have been a simple business morning when he inexplicably found himself in a Japan from another reality or time.

Some have also proposed that he may have been part of a **failed government experiment** involving interdimensional travel, in which he was accidentally transported into our dimension. However, there is no evidence to support this theory beyond pure speculation.

A Case of Conspiracy or Error

Of course, there is no shortage of sceptics who have tried to find more earthly explanations for the case of the Taured man. Some suggest that the whole story may have been a **hoax** or even a **journalistic fabrication** that eventually became an urban legend. While there is no direct evidence to support this claim, it is true that many details of the case cannot be confirmed by official sources. There are no clear public records of the man's disappearance or detailed reports of the incident in Japan's public archives.

Another possibility is that the man was simply a **victim of a mistake**: an immigrant with misinterpreted or falsified documents who was mistaken by the authorities in a moment of bewilderment. However, this does not explain how he disappeared from a locked room with surveillance, nor why his documents looked so legitimate, even though they came from a non-existent country.

The Legacy of Taured Man

Over the years, the story of the Taured Man has captured the imagination of many people, becoming a focal point in discussions of **alternate realities, parallel dimensions** and **time travel**. Although its authenticity has been debated, it remains an emblematic account among the unexplained cases of people who seem to have crossed the boundaries of reality as we know it.

Today, the Taured man is frequently mentioned in **conspiracy forums** and in books devoted to the paranormal. Although there are no clear answers, his story remains a fascinating reminder of how little we know about the true nature of time, space and reality itself.

Final Reflections

The case of the Taured man defies logical and rational explanation. Whether he was a traveller from an alternate reality, a man caught in a time slip, or simply an invention, we will never know for certain. However, his story remains one of the most enigmatic and puzzling accounts of the possibility that reality as we know it may not be as firm as we believe it to be.

10.2 Urban legends: Unconfirmed cases that refuse to go away

Over the years, numerous urban legends have circulated about alleged time travellers, stories that, without concrete evidence, have managed to capture the imagination of many people. Although unverified, these cases continue to be discussed in forums and debates, becoming modern myths that challenge our understanding of time and reality.

The man in the 1917 photograph with a "Swiss watch".

In **1973**, archaeologists unearthed a Ming Dynasty tomb in **Shanghai, China**. While excavating, they found a ring with a very particular shape. After cleaning it and examining it further, they discovered that what looked like the markings of a jewel was actually a **small Swiss watch** that read **10:06**. The mystery here is that, as far as is known, watches of this type did not exist until the 20th century.

This discovery sparked a wave of theories about how such an artefact could have found its way into a tomb more than 400 years old. Archaeologists were unable to find a satisfactory explanation for the presence of such an object in such an ancient excavation, fuelling speculation about time travellers inadvertently leaving evidence of its passage.

The legend of the "out of date" man in Liverpool

In **Liverpool**, England, there is an urban legend that tells of two friends meeting in an unusual situation in the 1990s. While walking through the city, one of the friends momentarily disappeared and, when he returned, claimed to have been in the **1950s**. According to his account, everything around him, including the buildings and people, had changed to that era.

This supposed traveller saw no time machines or technological artefacts, just a **complete transformation of the city** to what it would have looked like 40 years earlier. Although his friends initially took it as a joke, the detailed description of what he saw, from the shops to the cars, perfectly matched the appearance of Liverpool in the 1950s. The event is still the subject of speculation and has become one of the most talked about legends in the city.

The Los Angeles airport incident and the passenger with no past

Another curious case occurred at **Los Angeles airport** in the late 1990s. A man who had arrived on an international flight was detained by the authorities because of a mismatch in his **identity**. Although he was carrying a valid passport and other documents that appeared to be authentic, there was no record of him in the immigration systems.

The man seemed genuinely puzzled when the officers informed him that his country of origin, called **Belancia**, did not exist. Despite his attempts to explain where he came from, they were unable to find any information about the country in question or his existence. After being temporarily housed in a nearby hotel while they investigated, he disappeared without a trace. This case was never solved and fuelled the belief that he may have been an accidental traveller from another dimension.

The mysterious "tunnel traveller" in Chile

In **2008**, a driver in Chile was the subject of a story that quickly became a local legend. While driving along a road near the city of **Valparaíso**, he entered a tunnel in the highway and, according to his testimony, when he emerged from the tunnel, he found himself in a completely different version of the landscape he had left behind. The buildings were gone, the road was dirt, and the landscape looked like something out of an earlier era, with horses and carriages instead of automobiles.

The driver, confused and frightened, tried to return to the tunnel he had entered, but was unable to find it. Finally, hours after driving, he emerged in a nearby town. Although many dismiss this story as a hallucination, others believe that the driver may have passed through some sort of **temporal anomaly** that briefly transported him to another time.

The phone call of the future in Germany

In **1999**, a telecommunications operator in **Bonn, Germany**, received a strange call. Instead of hearing the voice of a normal customer, what she heard was a voice speaking in **old German**, using a slang that had fallen into disuse centuries ago. The call came from a non-existent number, and the most disconcerting thing was that it seemed to come from a phone located in **Bonn**, but in a place that no longer existed.

Some investigators who examined the case suggested that it could have been a technical interference or an electronic trick. For others, however, this call could have been evidence of a momentary contact with a person living in a different time, caught in some kind of **time slip**.

The man with the "one-way ticket".

In the 1990s, in a train station in **Milan**, Italy, a story about a man trying to buy a train ticket became an urban legend. The man, confused and distressed, tried to buy a ticket to a city that did not exist on any current rail route or map. Despite his insistence, the man was unable to convince station employees of the existence of this city. Legend has it that the man disappeared from the station without a trace, and was never seen again. Although the story has been debunked several times, it continues to circulate as an example of travellers who may have been out of time or from an alternate universe.

The call from the Titanic

Urban legend has it that, in **1970**, a woman in England received a strange phone call late at night. As she answered, she heard a man claiming to be part of the crew of the **Titanic**, calling for help as he described the desperate situation on board the sinking ship. The woman, though puzzled, listened to the call carefully until the line abruptly went dead. Despite attempts to trace the origin of the call, no evidence was found that it came from an existing phone. This story has become a curiosity that some interpret as a case of contact with the past through modern communication lines.

The mysterious lift man in Buenos Aires

In **1983**, a woman in **Buenos Aires**, Argentina, claimed to have had a surreal encounter in the lift of her building. As she was going up to the top floor, a man dressed in early 20th century clothing entered the lift. Although they exchanged few words, the man seemed completely out of place. According to the story, upon reaching the top floor, the man said goodbye and disappeared into thin air as he exited the lift, leaving the woman in shock. Years later, after investigating the building, the woman discovered that, decades earlier, a man of the same description had been the former owner of the place. This legend has been retold and transformed over the years, fuelling the belief in encounters with travellers from the past.

The traveller from the future at the 1996 Olympics

During the **Atlanta Olympics in 1996**, several people reported seeing a man wearing a very peculiar and futuristic outfit, with dark glasses and a kind of headset that did not correspond to the technology of the time. The man was seen by several witnesses at different events, but suddenly disappeared before anyone could interview or identify him. Many have interpreted this as a sighting of a traveller from the future who had decided to visit one of the most important events of the decade.

The boy who appeared on a train in Berlin

In the 1980s, a disconcerting case occurred in Berlin. A small boy was found alone and crying on a train running between stations. The strange thing about the case was that the child spoke an archaic German dialect that had fallen into disuse centuries ago. Despite efforts to find out his identity and how he got there, the authorities were never able to identify the child or find traces of his family. Eventually, some suggested that the boy had been the victim of a **time slip**, appearing at the wrong time.

Disappearance in the Mexican metro

A peculiar case occurred in the **Mexico City metro** in the 1960s. A young woman mysteriously disappeared after boarding a metro carriage. Witnesses claimed to have seen her enter the carriage, but she was never seen leaving, and when authorities checked security cameras, there was no trace of the woman at any other station. What made this case fuel theories of time travel is that the young woman was allegedly seen, decades later, in the same underground car, dressed exactly as she was on the day of her disappearance, although she was still young, as if she had not aged.

The case of the futuristic clock in the Arctic

In 1947, a group of British researchers exploring the Arctic regions made a disturbing discovery. They found a frozen corpse next to an object that appeared to be a wristwatch with a very advanced technology for the time. Although the watch did not correspond to the known designs of that decade, historical records describe it as a strange piece that could have come from the future. Although the story was not officially corroborated, it continues to circulate as an urban legend suggesting that the explorer may have been a time traveller who died in the attempt.

Final reflections

Urban legends about time travel continue to capture the collective imagination, offering an entry point for mystery and speculation. Although most lack supporting evidence, these stories continue to be discussed and shared, perhaps because they touch on one of the deepest human desires: to understand time and challenge its limitations.

Chapter 11: Science, Fiction and Time Paradoxes: Is Time Travel Possible?

Time travel is one of the most fascinating ideas mankind has ever conceived. While in fiction it has served as the basis for countless tales of adventure and paradox, in modern science it has become a subject of profound study. In this chapter we will explore how current science approaches the concept of time travel, what scientific theories underpin it, and how close or far we are from achieving it. In addition, we will address the temporal paradoxes that arise from modifying the past and how science fiction has shaped our ideas about this possibility.

11.1 Current scientific theories: Wormholes, relativity and multiverse

Current scientific theories that could enable time travel are based on some of the most fundamental principles of modern physics. Although time travel remains more of a theoretical than a practical possibility, physicists have formulated several hypotheses based on general relativity, quantum mechanics and cosmology. In the following, we will explore three key approaches: **wormholes**, **relativity** and the idea of the **multiverse**.

Wormholes: Space-time tunnels

The concept of wormholes arises from the solutions to the equations of **general relativity** proposed by Albert Einstein and Nathan Rosen in 1935, which led to them also being known as **Einstein-Rosen bridges**. These theoretical wormholes are tunnels that connect two points in space-time, allowing one to travel between them faster than travelling through "normal" space. In theory, if one of these points were in the past and one in the future, a wormhole would allow not only travel between different locations, but also between different times.

However, the main problem with wormholes is their instability. These theoretical tunnels would quickly collapse if any particle or radiation tried to pass through them. To keep a wormhole open and traversable, scientists believe it would be necessary to use **exotic matter** with **negative energy** properties. Such exotic matter has not been observed in nature, although some ideas have been proposed based on quantum phenomena, such as the **Casimir effect**, where two closely spaced metal plates create a small amount of negative energy between them.

The **challenge of causality** is another problematic aspect of wormholes. If they were possible, they would allow us to go back in time, which could create all sorts of **temporal paradoxes**, such as the famous grandfather paradox. For this reason, some scientists suggest that there may be laws of physics that prevent these paradoxes or, if they were to happen, would lead to the creation of a new parallel universe to avoid breaking the temporal coherence in our universe (more on this in the multiverse section).

Furthermore, the existence of **singularities** inside wormholes could have unpredictable effects on any object attempting to pass through them. Current theories suggest that any matter attempting to cross a wormhole could be destroyed by the **tidal forces** within the singularity. While science fiction has popularised wormholes as tools for time travel, in practice, we face enormous physical and technological limitations in making such travel a reality.

Relativity: Time, a malleable concept

Albert Einstein's **theory of** special and general **relativity** revolutionised our understanding of time and space, showing that they are not absolute but relative to the observer. This means that time can dilate or compress depending on conditions such as velocity and gravity. This malleability of time opens a theoretical door to **travel into the future**.

One of the most notable examples is **time dilation**, a phenomenon in which time passes more slowly for an object moving at speeds close to the speed of light. A classic example is the so-called **twin paradox**, in which one twin travels to a distant star in a ship moving at close to the speed of light, while the other twin stays on Earth. When the travelling twin returns, he or she discovers that he or she has aged much less than his or her sibling due to time dilation.

This effect is not just theoretical. In the 1970s, the **Hafele-Keating experiment** placed atomic clocks aboard aircraft flying around the Earth in opposite directions. By comparing these clocks with a clock that remained on Earth, it was found that the moving clocks showed a small but measurable time dilation, demonstrating that time really does run at a different rate depending on the relative speed.

Another related concept is **gravitational time dilation**, which occurs near objects with **huge gravitational fields**, such as black holes. The closer you are to a massive object, the slower time will pass for you compared to someone further away. A famous example of this phenomenon is shown in the film **"Interstellar"**, where one hour on a planet near a black hole is equivalent to several years on Earth.

However, travelling back in time using these principles is much more complicated. In order to go back in time, we would need to find a way to overcome the limitations of **causality** and possible paradoxes, something that has not yet been solved by current physics.

Multiverse: Infinite timelines

The **multiverse** is one of the most speculative, but also one of the most attractive theories in the field of time travel. Proposed in part by the **many-worlds interpretation** of quantum mechanics, the multiverse idea suggests that every time a major decision or event occurs, the universe splits, creating a new parallel universe with a different outcome. This implies that there are infinite universes with infinite variations of reality.

In the context of time travel, the multiverse theory offers a possible solution to **temporal paradoxes**. If one were to travel back in time and change a significant event, instead of affecting one's own timeline, one could simply create a new timeline in a parallel universe. This would mean that time travellers would not have to worry about creating paradoxes, as any changes would only affect the new reality they have created.

In addition, some physicists suggest that the **multiverse** could be a solution to the causality problems found in more conventional theories of time travel. If every time you change something in the past you simply jump to a new universe, paradoxes would be avoided, as each universe would follow its own course.

One of the biggest challenges for the multiverse theory is that, so far, we have not found a way to test its existence. It is a difficult theory to experiment with or prove directly, as we do not have access to these parallel universes. However, **string theory** and **inflationary cosmology** suggest that the multiverse could be real, and if we can one day prove it, we could open the door not only to time travel, but also to travel between different realities.

11.2 Time paradoxes: What happens if you change the past?

Temporal paradoxes represent one of the most complex conceptual obstacles in the study of time travel. If it were possible to travel back in time, what would happen if we changed a major event? These questions have fascinated science fiction writers and theoretical physicists alike, as any significant alteration could create contradictions that defy logic and causality. Let's look at some of the best-known paradoxes and how they have been attempted to be resolved theoretically.

The grandfather paradox

The **grandfather paradox** is probably the most famous paradox when discussing time travel. The scenario is simple: if a time traveller returns to the past and kills his grandfather before he has children, how could the traveller himself have been born? This creates a logical cycle in which the act of changing the past seems self-annulling, since if the grandfather dies, the traveller could never have existed to commit the murder.

This paradox poses a dilemma about **causality**: how can the present and the past coexist if a change in the past destroys the present that led to the change? This is where many physicists and philosophers have proposed various theoretical solutions:

1. **Parallel Universe Theory**: According to this solution, when a traveller changes the past, it does not affect their own original timeline. Instead, **a new timeline**, or parallel universe, is created in which history follows a different course. Thus, the traveller who kills his grandfather moves to a new timeline where he is never born, but his existence in his original timeline remains intact. This idea has been used in many works of science fiction, such as the Marvel comic book stories or the BACK TO THE FUTURE film series.
2. **Self-consistency theory**: According to this hypothesis, any event that a traveller attempts to alter in the past is already "written" in history in a way that cannot be changed. In other words, even if you tried to kill your grandfather, something

would prevent you from doing so: the weapon might misfire, you might regret it at the last moment, or somehow events would be rearranged to maintain the consistency of the original timeline. This suggests that the past is immutable and that paradoxes cannot be generated. This idea is explored in works such as Isaac Asimov's novel THE END OF ETERNITY.

Paradoxes of causality

Another fascinating category of temporal paradoxes are **causality paradoxes**, which arise when a future event causes a past event, creating a closed causal cycle where there appears to be no clear origin for the events. A classic example of this is known as the **information paradox** or **predestination paradox**.

A typical example of a causality paradox is the story of the musician who receives a musical score from a person who travels back in time, and the musician plays the score. The musician plays the score and then, many years later, meets the time traveller and gives him the same score. Where did the music originally come from? There is no clear origin of the information here, as it seems to pass in a cycle without an original creator.

Another famous example is that of a person who travels into the past to give their younger self the answer to a complicated problem, as mentioned in the paradox of the answer sheet. The cycle becomes a logical loop where the future and the past feed back into each other, but there is no clear initial cause for that information to exist.

Such paradoxes are not only challenging in science fiction, but also present problems for the laws of physics. **Causality** is one of the fundamental principles in physics, and any violation of causality could have profound implications for our understanding of the universe.

Novikov's self-consistent consistency

One of the possible solutions to temporal paradoxes is the proposal of Russian physicist **Igor Novikov**, called **Novikov's self-consistent consistency conjecture**. This theory suggests that the universe is structured in such a way that paradoxes are impossible. Instead of allowing changes in the past to generate contradictions, the course of events themselves would naturally rearrange themselves to prevent this from happening.

An example of this theory is that, if a time traveller tries to kill his grandfather, something will inevitably prevent him from doing so.

Perhaps the weapon jams or misfires at the crucial moment, or perhaps the traveller gets distracted and changes his mind. Any attempt to alter the past would be **predestined** to fail, ensuring that history remains coherent. Thus, although the traveller can interact with the past, he or she cannot change anything significantly.

This theory attempts to preserve the **coherence** of the timeline without resorting to parallel universes or new timelines. If the past cannot be changed, then temporal paradoxes, such as the grandfather paradox, have no place, since the traveller could never change an important event. This idea has been explored in several works of science fiction, such as the episode "**The Constant**" from the series "LOST".

Other known time paradoxes

Apart from the three main paradoxes mentioned above, there are other ideas related to time travel that also present interesting complications:

The paradox of predestination:

This paradox implies that any attempt to change the past is not only futile, but is destined to comply with already established events. In this case, the time traveller might believe that he is altering the course of history, but in reality, he is playing a role in the inevitable unfolding of those same events. This suggests that the time traveller's actions are already part of the fabric of history that he himself is trying to modify.

A classic example of the paradox of predestination is the plot of the film 12 MONKEYS (1995), where the protagonist travels back in time to prevent a global disaster, only to discover that his actions in the past are what ultimately contribute to the event he was trying to prevent. In this case, everything is "fated" to happen the same way, and the time traveller cannot escape that fate.

The closed causal loop

Another interesting paradox related to causality is the concept of a **closed causal loop**, where cause and effect feed back into each other in an endless cycle. In this scenario, an object or information can "exist" without having a clear origin. This idea defies the usual logic, where every cause has an effect and every effect has a cause.

An example of this is the idea of receiving crucial information from the future. Imagine that a scientist receives a detailed blueprint of a time machine from his future self. He uses the blueprint to build the machine, which later allows him to travel back in time and give that same blueprint to his younger self. Here, the blueprint never had a clear origin, as it is transferred in an infinite cycle between the future and the past without having been created in the first place.

Such causal loops have been explored in several science fiction stories, such as in the film PREDESTINATION (2014), where a temporal agent follows an endless cycle of cause and effect, which becomes increasingly confusing as he tries to unravel his own identity.

The observer's paradox

A lesser-known version of temporal paradoxes is the **observer paradox**, which refers to the inconsistencies that can arise when a time traveller observes events without directly intervening. In this case, merely witnessing an event in the past could unpredictably alter the course of history.

The observer paradox is related to the **quantum interpretation of the observer**, where the act of observing a system can change its state. In the context of time travel, the presence of the traveller, even if not directly interacting with events, could subtly change circumstances, generating a butterfly effect. This raises questions about how time travellers could influence the past without even realising they are doing so.

Are time paradoxes avoidable?

Over the years, physicists have tried to formulate theories that allow time travel without falling into paradox traps. In addition to **Novikov's self-consistent consistency**, there are other theories that explore ways to avoid paradoxes, such as the **multiverse theory** mentioned above.

Some scientists argue that time paradoxes only exist in theoretical scenarios and that physical reality has natural mechanisms to prevent them from occurring. For example, **wormholes**, if they existed, could lead to other timelines or parallel realities, where the changes would not affect the original traveller's past. This would imply that, even if time travel is possible, there would be no paradox because the traveller would be creating a new reality with every action he or she takes.

Another possibility is that there are **laws of nature** that we do not yet fully understand that could prevent paradoxes. For example, some physicists speculate that **black holes** or certain quantum phenomena could act as "time keepers", preventing the traveller's actions from affecting his or her own past or altering causality dramatically.

Final Reflection: The Limits of Paradox in Modern Physics

As modern science continues to advance, physicists are constantly re-evaluating the implications of time travel. Although time paradoxes pose fascinating conceptual challenges, most of them remain matters of theoretical speculation rather than actual physical problems. Studies in **relativity** and **quantum mechanics** have shown that time is much more flexible than humans used to imagine, but we are still far from fully understanding its limits.

While paradoxes such as grandfather paradoxes or causal loops are intriguing obstacles in the discussion of time travel, they may be mere theoretical exercises that will never find their correspondence in the physical world. For now, time paradoxes remain one of the biggest challenges for those trying to reconcile the possibility of time travel with the consistency of physical laws.

Conclusion:

The **paradox of time** not only challenges our understanding of the universe, but also invites reflection on the very nature of reality and causality. While science continues to investigate how time might work at the quantum and cosmic level, paradoxes such as the grandfather paradox, the predestination paradox and causal loops remain as reminders of how complex our relationship with time is. As our technology advances and physical theories develop, perhaps one day we will discover ways to travel through time without falling into these logical traps.

11.3 Is time travel possible? What science says today

Time travel has fascinated both scientists and philosophers throughout history. Although there is still no practical way to travel through time in the way that science fiction depicts it, some well-founded physical theories suggest that it is not impossible. Special relativity, general relativity, wormholes and black holes, among other phenomena, offer intriguing insights that bring us closer to a deeper understanding of how time travel might work.

Time dilation: A small but real example

Time dilation is one of the most direct evidence that time is not an immutable constant. According to Einstein's **theory of special**

relativity, time passes more slowly for objects moving at speeds close to the speed of light compared to observers at rest. This means that, under certain extreme conditions, time can behave in very different ways from what we usually experience.

One of the most famous experiments demonstrating this effect is the **Hafele-Keating experiment**, conducted in 1971. Scientists Hafele and Keating placed extremely accurate atomic clocks aboard planes that flew around the world in opposite directions. When they compared these clocks with one that had remained on the ground, they found that the clocks on the planes showed slight differences in elapsed time. The clock that moved faster (at a higher speed) had experienced time dilation: time passed more slowly for it compared to the clock at rest on Earth.

Although this effect is minuscule in our everyday lives, it has enormous implications when taken to near-light speeds. If a spacecraft could travel at 99.9% of the speed of light, the occupants of the spacecraft would experience time much more slowly than observers on Earth. In theory, an astronaut travelling for a few years at this speed could return to Earth to find that centuries have passed. This phenomenon, called **relativistic future travel**, is a type of time travel that has already been observed and measured, albeit only on very small scales.

Wormholes: Hypothetical bridges to other times

Wormholes, also known as Einstein-Rosen bridges, are a theoretical solution to the equations of **general relativity** that describe shortcuts through space-time. A wormhole could connect two distant points in space, or even two points in time, opening up the possibility of travelling through different epochs.

However, these wormholes present enormous challenges. One of the most difficult problems to solve is their stability. Wormholes, according to current equations, tend to collapse rapidly as soon as any particle (ordinary matter) tries to pass through them. To keep a wormhole open, theoretical physicists have proposed that **exotic matter** with negative energy properties would be needed. This exotic matter would be able to counteract the gravitational forces that would collapse the wormhole, but so far we have found no concrete evidence for its existence.

Another problem with wormholes is **causality**. If they could be used to travel into the past, they could generate temporal paradoxes, such as the famous grandfather paradox. Some scientists speculate that there may be natural laws of physics that prevent travel into the past in order to preserve the coherence of causality. Still, wormholes remain one of the most fascinating theoretical propositions, and many physicists continue to study whether they might one day be feasible.

Black holes and event horizons

Another intriguing idea is that **black holes** could offer a natural way to "travel into the future". Black holes are regions of space where gravity is so intense that even light cannot escape its influence. In the vicinity of a black hole, extreme gravity distorts both space and time, resulting in **gravitational time dilation**.

Near a black hole, especially in the vicinity of its **event horizon** (the region beyond which nothing can escape), time slows down enormously compared to the time experienced far from the black hole. If an observer were in the vicinity of a black hole for what for him would be only a few minutes, he could return to a region further away and discover that for the rest of the universe, decades or even centuries have passed. Such a journey into the future is a real possibility according to the laws of general relativity.

However, black holes are not a safe option for time travellers. Any object crossing the event horizon of a black hole would face gravitational forces so intense that it would inevitably be destroyed by **tidal forces**, a phenomenon known as **spaghettification**. These forces would stretch and crush any spacecraft or humans that tried to get too close. While it is tempting to think that black holes might offer a way into the future, the extreme conditions make this possibility unfeasible for travellers.

Beyond Theoretical: Technical Challenges

Although the ideas of **time dilation**, **wormholes** and **black holes** suggest possible avenues for time travel, we are still a long way from realising these theories. The technological and physical challenges are immense. Reaching near-light speeds would require colossal amounts of energy, and the creation of stable wormholes remains a distant dream.

In addition, studies on **quantum mechanics** and **quantum gravity** are still in their early stages. Theoretical physicists are exploring how general relativity could be unified with quantum mechanics, which could reveal new insights into the nature of time and space. **Quantum gravity** could provide clues as to whether time travel is possible without falling into paradoxes or breaking the laws of causality.

11.4 Is science closer to unlocking the secrets of time travel?

Science has made giant strides in understanding the nature of time, but we are still a long way from finding a practical way to travel through it. However, developments in **quantum mechanics**, **quantum gravity** and **theoretical physics** are pushing the boundaries of our understanding, and could offer clues about how to manipulate time in the future. Below, we explore two key areas of research that are beginning to bring us closer to the theoretical possibility of time travel.

Quantum entanglement and causality

Quantum entanglement is one of the most mysterious and fascinating phenomena in quantum mechanics. When two particles are entangled, their states are connected in such a way that any change in one particle instantly affects the other, no matter how far apart they are. This phenomenon was described by Albert Einstein as "phantom action at a distance", as it seems to violate the classical notion of causality, which states that no information or influence can travel faster than light.

This entanglement raises profound questions about **causality** and the flow of time. On a quantum level, it appears that effects can precede causes, suggesting that, under certain conditions, the rules of time may not be as strict as we think. Some scientists have speculated that, in the future, we may discover ways to harness quantum entanglement to manipulate time or even travel through it.

However, one of the main problems with quantum entanglement is that, although the particles are instantaneously correlated, there does not seem to be any way to use this correlation to transmit useful information or to travel through time in a practical way. The phenomenon appears to be limited to the quantum scale, and any attempt to use entanglement to alter the past or the future is still beyond our reach.

Despite these limitations, some theoretical physicists believe that quantum entanglement could be an indicator that, at a fundamental level, time and space are more flexible than we imagine. This has led to speculation about the role of **quantum gravity** in manipulating time.

Quantum gravity and wormholes

One of the greatest challenges in modern physics is the unification of **quantum mechanics** with the **theory of general relativity**. While general relativity describes how gravity shapes space-time on a cosmic scale, quantum mechanics deals with phenomena on the smallest scales of the universe. So far, these two theories have been incredibly successful in their respective domains, but they have not been fully reconciled with each other. **Quantum gravity** is the field that seeks to unify these two theories, and in the process, could unlock fundamental secrets about the nature of time.

One of the most interesting scenarios to emerge from some **quantum gravity** models is the possibility that **wormholes** exist at the quantum level. According to some theories, wormholes could be a natural consequence of the quantum fluctuation of space-time. In other words, small wormholes could constantly open and close on a microscopic scale. Although these wormholes would be incredibly small and ephemeral, some scientists speculate that, under certain conditions, they could stabilise and expand enough to allow matter or information to pass through.

One of the biggest problems we face in trying to use these quantum wormholes for time travel is the **negative energy** needed to keep them open. Theory suggests that to prevent the wormholes from collapsing, we would need to use a form of energy that counteracts gravitational forces. So far, this negative energy has only been observed in very limited experiments and in controlled situations, such as the **Casimir effect**, but we do not know if it could be used practically on a large scale.

Furthermore, the concept of **quantum foam**, a structure in which space-time is constantly fluctuating, suggests that space-time itself could be malleable at the quantum level. Some theoretical physicists, such as Stephen Hawking, speculated that if we could understand and manipulate this quantum foam, we could open the door to time travel through quantum wormholes. However, we are far from having the technology or knowledge to experiment with these concepts on a practical level.

The limits of modern physics

Despite theoretical advances in quantum physics and relativity, the main obstacle to unlocking the secrets of time remains the lack of a **complete theory of quantum gravity**. Current proposals, such as **string theory** or **loop quantum gravity**, offer possible explanations for how space-time behaves at the quantum level, but have not yet been tested experimentally. Without a complete understanding of how the universe works on these scales, any attempt to manipulate time remains highly speculative.

In addition, there are inherent limits to how we can experiment with time. At the quantum level, the Heisenberg **uncertainty principle** imposes restrictions on our ability to accurately measure certain aspects of time and space. This principle suggests that there will always be a level of unpredictability in our observations, which could make control over time impossible to achieve.

What does the future hold?

Despite current challenges, modern physics is at a crossroads. Research in **quantum gravity**, **wormholes** and **quantum entanglement** offer us glimpses of a future in which we may discover how to manipulate time. Although we are far from time travel in the way we imagine in science fiction, each step we take towards understanding these phenomena brings us closer to unlocking the secrets of the universe.

In the end, time may be much more flexible than we once thought. Science still has much to discover about the true nature of time and space, and advances in quantum and theoretical physics may open new doors in the future. In the meantime, theories about time remain one of the most fascinating and speculative fields in modern science.

Chapter 12: Conclusion: Myths, Realities and the Future of Time Travel

Time travel is one of the most challenging concepts ever conceived by humankind. From its earliest hints in mythology to its deep exploration in science fiction and modern scientific theories, it has been an idea that has challenged the frontiers of our understanding of the universe. Being able to jump from one era to another, manipulate historical events or glimpse into the future has fascinated philosophers, scientists and authors for generations.

From the myth of Chronos, which personifies time as a devouring titan, to modern tales that explore the complexities of temporal paradoxes, time has always been seen as immutable and uncontrollable. And yet, the possibility of defying this barrier, of stepping outside temporal constraints and navigating freely through different epochs, is a fantasy deeply rooted in the human mind.

Science, for its part, has played a crucial role in keeping this possibility alive. With Einstein's theory of relativity and the concept of wormholes, physics has suggested that we may not be as time-bound as we once thought. Although current technological advances do not allow us to make time jumps, the doors to this possibility remain ajar. Quantum physics has challenged our perceptions of reality, suggesting that time may be far more flexible and malleable than we imagine.

The fascination with time travel is not simply a scientific question, but also an emotional and philosophical one. Time affects us all inexorably: the passage of time brings with it ageing, the loss of loved ones, the end of opportunities and uncertainty about what is to come. In a world where time is linear and constant, being able to manipulate it could mean freedom over these seemingly inevitable aspects of our lives. It would allow us to relive happy moments, correct mistakes or avoid tragedies. In short, it would touch on one of the most universal human desires: control over our destiny.

But at the same time, time travel also raises complex and disturbing questions. If we could change the past, who would decide which events should be altered? What would be the consequences in the present if someone altered a crucial historical event? And, perhaps more disturbingly, what happens to personal identity when time is manipulated? If the past can be changed, is one still the same person?

The debate about time travel also extends to the ethical plane. Suppose it were possible to travel back in time and avoid catastrophes, what would be the moral repercussions of altering historical events? Would we be doomed to create a present where even worse tragedies have taken place? These questions are the fuel for many science fiction stories, but also for deeper philosophical discussions about destiny, freedom and the role of human beings in the universe.

Another important aspect to consider is how popular culture has shaped our perception of time. Through books, films and television series, we have been bombarded with different versions of the future and the past. Stories like BACK TO THE FUTURE or INTERSTELLAR not only entertain us, but also invite us to seriously consider the implications of time travel. In many cases, science fiction has anticipated science itself, offering a vision of what might be possible in the distant future.

The concept of time and the possibility of travelling through it brings us face to face with a crucial question: what is time in reality? Is it a dimension like space, which can be navigated? Or is it something immutable, a stream that flows only in one direction? These questions are some of the most profound that theoretical physics is trying to resolve, and their answer could change our understanding of reality itself.

While time travel remains a mystery, science has advanced far enough to suggest that we may not be that far away from understanding it. While it may seem unattainable, we should not forget that, just a few centuries ago, flying through the sky or communicating instantaneously across vast distances were equally fantastic concepts. Scientific progress has a way of transforming the impossible into the plausible.

So while time travel may be a distant horizon, the fact that we continue to explore it in our minds, through scientific theories and fictional accounts, is a testament to our ongoing quest to unravel the deepest mysteries of the universe. Is it possible that time travel will one day become a reality? For now, we can only dream and speculate, but science continues to open small windows of possibility, giving us a glimpse that perhaps time is not as rigid as we thought.

12.1 Reflection on why we continue to be fascinated by time travel

The fascination with time travel is much more than just a yearning for impossible adventures or a curiosity for the unknown. At its core, it reflects one of the most universal and deep-rooted human desires: control over destiny. Since time immemorial, human beings have sought to understand, control and manipulate the forces that govern their lives. In this quest, time has been presented as one of the most mysterious and immovable forces, which has fuelled an obsession with imagining what we could do if we had the power to move backwards or forwards in time.

The desire to change the past

One of the most obvious reasons why time travel fascinates us is the desire to change the past. We have all experienced moments when we would like to go back, whether to correct a mistake, make a different decision or simply relive a moment of happiness. The idea that we might get a second chance at life, or that we might undo something we regret, is deeply appealing. Regret, as an emotion, can be a heavy burden, and the possibility of relieving that burden by changing the course of past events is something that resonates in virtually every culture and time.

This desire is reflected in many science fiction stories and literary works throughout history. From Charles Dickens' classic tale in A CHRISTMAS CAROL, where Ebenezer Scrooge is given the opportunity to see how his life could change if he changed his behaviour, to films such as BACK TO THE FUTURE, the theme of altering the past to right wrongs is a recurring one. The narrative of "a second chance" strikes an emotional chord in all of us.

The yearning to explore the future

At the other extreme, the fascination with the future is equally powerful. The future is an unknown, a space where our ambitions, fears and hopes are projected. We are intrigued by the possibility of knowing what will happen to us and to the world. How will humanity evolve? What technological or scientific advances will be made? What will the society of the future look like? These are questions we have all asked ourselves at one time or another.

The journey into the future also feeds our thirst for adventure and discovery. Just as the explorers of the past wanted to discover unknown lands, we long to explore what is to come. However, this yearning is not without ambiguity: the future can also be terrifying. Dystopian representations of the future, as in novels such as George Orwell's 1984 or Aldous Huxley's BRAVE NEW WORLD, show how this desire to know the future can also reveal a dark mirror of our own current concerns.

Science fiction as a cultural catalyst

Science fiction has undoubtedly been one of the most important drivers behind this fascination. From the earliest accounts of time travel in 19th century literature to today's films and television series, science fiction has shaped our perception of what is possible. Works such as H.G. Wells' THE TIME MACHINE, Christopher Nolan's INTERSTELLAR or series such as DOCTOR WHO have expanded the limits of our imagination by positing different theories, paradoxes and scenarios revolving around time.

The interesting thing about science fiction is that, although its stories are often anchored in fantasy, they often touch on deep philosophical themes about human nature. Time travel not only serves to entertain, but also opens the door to reflections on our responsibility for the past, the consequences of our actions and the importance of the present. These stories not only show us the wonders we might find in other times, but also the ethical dilemmas and complexities that arise when we play with time.

The influence of science

As science has advanced, it has fed this obsession in a more tangible way. Albert Einstein's theories of special relativity and general relativity have revealed that time is not a universal constant, but can be stretched or compressed under certain conditions. This suggests that, under the right circumstances, it may be possible to alter our experience of time.

Although theories of wormholes and time dilation are far from being proven in practice, they have offered a scientific basis for the possibility that, in the future, time travel may cease to be a fantasy and become a reality. Science has done what mythology and religion could not: offer hope that, perhaps, time can be manipulated in ways we do not yet fully understand.

Hope, curiosity and the impossible

The fascination with time travel also reflects a more philosophical part of our nature: the constant search for the impossible. Throughout history, humankind has achieved accomplishments once thought unattainable. From flying to sending probes to distant planets, we have achieved what past generations could only dream of. Time travel represents, in a sense, the next "impossible" that we long to conquer. It is a reflection of our infinite curiosity and our ability to imagine beyond the limits of reality.

Ultimately, time travel, whether possible or not, will continue to be a subject that captures our imagination. As we continue to explore the frontiers of science, and as our narratives about time continue to evolve, the possibility of breaking through time barriers will remain a symbol of our eternal struggle to understand the universe and our place in it.

12.2 What does the future hold in this field?

The future of time travel, though still shrouded in mystery, is closer to being explored than ever before. Science is advancing at an astonishing pace, and concepts that once seemed exclusively out of science fiction are now being seriously debated in theoretical and quantum physics. Although we are far from building a time machine like the one we see in the movies, scientific discoveries have opened doors to new possibilities that could, in the future, unlock some of the universe's greatest secrets.

Wormholes: The Bridge to the Future (or the Past)

One of the most exciting concepts in theoretical physics is that of wormholes, hypothetical tunnels connecting distant points in space-time. If they were stable, they could act as a kind of "shortcut" through time, allowing instantaneous travel between two distant times or places. Wormholes offer a fascinating theoretical route to the past or future, but their stability is a major obstacle: they would need a form of negative energy to avoid collapsing, something that has not yet been observed in nature in a practical way.

Despite this, the mere possibility that such shortcuts exist raises exciting questions: could humanity one day find a way to stabilise wormholes? If we succeed, we could be standing at the door that would allow us to move through time and space in ways we can't even imagine today.

Relativity: A step towards time manipulation

Einstein's theory of relativity has shown us that time is not a universal constant, but can be influenced by gravity and velocity. Time dilation, where time passes more slowly for a fast-moving object or near a large source of gravity, has already been observed in small experiments with atomic clocks. Although time dilation does not represent time travel in a meaningful way, it demonstrates that time is much more flexible than previously thought.

If in the future we succeed in developing technologies that allow humans to reach near-light speeds or interact with extreme sources of gravity, such as black holes, we could be closer to travelling into the future, where time for travellers would run differently from the rest of the universe.

The future of quantum mechanics: New ways of understanding time

Quantum mechanics has revolutionised our understanding of reality, challenging our perceptions of what is possible. Quantum phenomena, such as entanglement, suggest that particles can be connected across vast distances in a way that defies classical causality. Although these phenomena have not yet been fully understood, some scientists believe they may offer clues to the manipulation of time at the quantum level.

Quantum gravity, a developing theory that seeks to unify relativity with quantum mechanics, could be the key to opening new doors in our understanding of time. Some theories speculate that wormholes could exist at the quantum level and, under certain conditions, could expand enough to allow matter to pass through. While this sounds like pure science fiction today, the history of science is full of examples where seemingly impossible ideas have become tangible realities.

The horizon of the unknown: what lies ahead

It is possible that in the distant future, time travel will no longer be a fantasy. Perhaps we will discover how to manipulate quantum particles or stabilise wormholes, allowing people to travel through time and space. While we don't yet have clear answers, each new scientific breakthrough brings us a little closer to this possibility.

The questions that arise from the potential of time travel also invite us to reflect on its ethical and philosophical implications: what if it were possible to alter the past? What would be the consequences for the present and the future? Should we have the power to interfere with history, or is it too dangerous for the common good? These questions will not only be crucial in the scientific debates of the future, but also in the realm of philosophy and politics.

Conclusion: Myths, Realities and the Future of Time Travel

Time travel is a concept that has transcended the barriers of thought, evolving from ancient legends and myths to become a legitimate field of study within modern physics. Although science has not yet found a practical way to achieve it, advances in the understanding of space-time, relativity and quantum mechanics have begun to unravel the depths of this phenomenon.

The myths and realities surrounding time travel have pushed us to explore our relationship with time more deeply, not only scientifically, but also philosophically. As we continue to advance in our research, each new discovery, each new theory, brings us a little closer to the possibility that, one day, time can be mastered or manipulated.

Perhaps the biggest mystery is not whether we can travel back in time, but **how** we would do it and **what** the consequences would be. We face a field full of unanswered questions, but also unimaginable opportunities. The future of time travel, though uncertain, is as fascinating as the concept itself, and continues to drive scientists and dreamers alike to challenge the limits of what we think is possible.

So, although time travel is still on the horizon, science continues to explore its limits, challenging our perceptions of time, space and reality itself. With each discovery, we come closer to understanding the mysteries of the universe. Perhaps, in the not-so-distant future, we will master the secrets of time, transforming what was once just a dream into a new reality.

Bibliography

Scientific and Academic Works:

- Hawking, Stephen. A BRIEF HISTORY OF TIME. Bantam Books, 1988.
- Einstein, Albert. THE MEANING OF RELATIVITY. Princeton University Press, 1955.
- Carroll, Sean. FROM ETERNITY TO HERE: THE QUEST FOR THE ULTIMATE THEORY OF TIME. Dutton, 2010.
- Greene, Brian. THE FABRIC OF THE COSMOS: SPACE, TIME, AND THE TEXTURE OF REALITY. Vintage Books, 2004.
- Kaku, Michio. HYPERSPACE: A SCIENTIFIC ODYSSEY THROUGH PARALLEL UNIVERSES, TIME WARPS, AND THE 10TH DIMENSION. Anchor Books, 1994.
- Everett, Hugh. THE MANY-WORLDS INTERPRETATION OF QUANTUM MECHANICS. Princeton University Press, 1957.
- Thorne, Kip. BLACK HOLES AND TIME WARPS: EINSTEIN'S OUTRAGEOUS LEGACY. Norton, 1994.
- Tegmark, Max. OUR MATHEMATICAL UNIVERSE: MY QUEST FOR THE ULTIMATE NATURE OF REALITY. Knopf, 2014.
- Deutsch, David. THE FABRIC OF REALITY. Penguin Books, 1997.

Popular Culture:

- BACK TO THE FUTURE - Directed by Robert Zemeckis, 1985.
- TERMINATOR - Directed by James Cameron, 1984.
- DARK - Created by Baran bo Odar and Jantje Friese, 2017.
- STEINS;GATE - Directed by Hiroshi Hamasaki, 2011.
- ERASED - Directed by Tomohiko Itō, 2016.
- THE TIME MACHINE - H.G. Wells, William Heinemann, 1895.
- DOCTOR WHO - Created by Sydney Newman, BBC, 1963.

- THE BUTTERFLY EFFECT - Directed by Eric Bress and J. Mackye Gruber, 2004.
- INTERSTELLAR - Directed by Christopher Nolan, 2014.
- COAST TO COAST AM - Created by Art Bell.

ABOUT THE AUTHOR

Maximilian Cross is a dreamy author, fascinated by the mysteries of time and the impact of social structures on modern life. With a curious mind that travels beyond the obvious, he finds inspiration from his experiences around the world, exploring different cultures and landscapes. His interest in the global economy and how it affects people in their daily lives is reflected in his writings, where he addresses issues of social control, freedom and the search for a better future.

Passionate about film, Cross incorporates an almost cinematic vision into his stories, creating narratives that combine science, history and philosophy, with a touch of fantasy that challenges the boundaries of knowledge. His thoughtful, provocative and deeply imaginative style invites readers to question the realities we take for granted and to dream of the impossible.

I hope this book has been a window to new perspectives and that you dare to keep dreaming. Because in the end, great changes begin with those who dare to imagine the impossible.

Thank you!

Printed in Great Britain
by Amazon